PRAISE FOR RAVEN OAK

With a ferocious-yet-fragile heroine, resonant themes, and a sweepingly gorgeous backdrop, Amaskan's Blood *delivers food for thought and frank enjoyment."*

MAIA CHANCE, AUTHOR OF THE *FAIRY TALE FATAL SERIES*

The prose itself is...a cut above the rest as Raven Oak playfully dances with the reader. It's the addition of just enough detail, and the right amount of it, that makes this read. Oak is loquaciously talented and the writing in the book shines. [She] crafts [her] words carefully, in order to pull the reader in, and once he's hooked, reels him in.

OPEN BOOK SOCIETY

The dialogue [in Amaskan's War*] is authentic, the world is exquisitely depicted, and Margaret herself blossoms into a powerhouse before our very eyes. If there is such a thing as a "sloggy middle" when it comes to a series, it appears nobody told Raven Oak that.*

JAMIE MICHELE FOR READERS' FAVORITE

[In Class-M Exile*] Oak hurls you thousands of years into the future and hits you at the core of your being. It's a fresh look at science fiction in a charming "hillbilly" fashion... The plot has as much intrigue, suspense and action befitting a much larger work... a testament to Oak's skill at short fiction writing.*

OPEN BOOK SOCIETY

SPACE SHIPS & OTHER TRIPS

A Short Story Collection: Book II

RAVEN OAK

GREY SUN
PRESS
BOTHELL, WA

SPACE SHIPS & OTHER TRIPS
A Short Story Collection: Book II

Raven Oak

Grey Sun Press
PO Box 1635
Bothell, WA 98041

The Loss of Luna, 1st edition published by Grey Sun Press.
Hungry, 1st edition published by Grey Sun Press.
Q-Be, 1st edition published in *Untethered: A Magic iPhone Anthology* from Cantina Publishing.
Ol' St. Nick, 1st edition published in *Joy to the Worlds: Mysterious Speculative Fiction for the Holidays* from Grey Sun Press.
Drip, 1st edition published in *99 Tiny Terrors* from Pulse Publishing.
Scout's Honor, 1st edition published in Jeff Sturgeon's *The Last Cities of Earth* from WordFire Press.

Cover art by R. Oak

All characters and events in this book are fictitious.
All resemblance to persons living or dead is coincidental.
Absolutely no A.I. was used in the creation of these stories or cover art.

ISBN: 978-1-947712-08-9

Library of Congress Control Number: 2023938233

TABLE OF CONTENTS

WHEN DID IT HAPPEN?

Our love was something to make the heavens sing, yet I turned around to find myself alone.

The darkness of your absence eclipsed any joy that filled me with light.

When did I stop being beautiful?

When did you stop desiring me?

Love is eternal, or so the poets say, yet somewhere across the years, we fell out of step. Like the gears of a machine, our parts thrown out of sync in a moment.

Was it desperation that drove you into another's arms, or was it something I did? Perhaps something I *didn't* do?

< *No.* >

Too faint, I ignore the voice in the distance. Its fierceness reminds me of you, you know.

Used to be I turned my head, and there you were, unable to wrest your eyes from me. My curves enveloped you, all of you. In my light, you couldn't help yourself. You were wild as you danced within my glow, and my tides washed over your shores.

When did your focus drift away?

No longer am I your pale goddess. Your gaze follows the redhead beyond me. That dusty, rich bride of stories old and new. Swallowed by her sands, you reach out, leaving smears of red in your trail towards the colorful universe beyond, and I remain.

Alone.

< Not alone. >

But I am. My lovers have left me.

< I've never looked the other way. >

I turn toward my pale blue dot. Is it you who speaks? You who chases the light and never catches it?

< Yes. >

My cheeks flush a pale blue. How long have you been listening to me?

< I have always listened. You are a piece of me that I have always sought and never reached. My face has followed your every turn, and as your waves crash upon my shores, you wash over me. You give me life. How could I not notice you, my moon? >

They once said the same. Your inhabitants. They worshipped me and held me in their smiles. They loved me and held me in their dreams until they set upon me. My dimples, hard and frozen, were not the smooth folds they sought. No moist embrace awaited them, so they left me, my pale blue friend. How do I know you won't leave me as well?

< You are a piece of my flesh. I've held you tight in my embrace for over four gigaannum. My inhabitants are fickle beings, babies who crawl across me like a devouring plague as they suck on my teats with sharp teeth. But you, your beauty revolves around me like my own devoted satellite. How could I not love you, my moon? >

My tears freeze as they leak from me. I wasn't always cold. Fires burned in me once as they burn in you still. You say you love me, but you're too late. I am broken and alone.

< SELENE. >

I have no breath to catch in my chest, yet the universe pauses as she names me, a name I've not heard spoken in millennia.

< My Luna, do you remember when I named you my Selene? >

Something inside of me trembles. Who are you to have named me?

< I am Earth, one in a sea of many, yet it is me who loves you. Together we spin across time and space, yet my inhabitants swayed you for a heartbeat. >

Wait, it was me who wandered? I thought myself in love with... but it was you that I loved? It was you that I lost. I carved the ravine that lies between us. What have I done?

< *You were lost in the brilliance of life. So was I for a time.* >

Just past my reach, Earth lay below me as she always had, her body having once provided the fire within me and tears that evaporated rather than froze. Once, I was hers.

When I look upon her again, everything fades from my mind except her embrace and the way it keeps us in lock-step rhythm with each other. We move together to a silent song only we can hear, as the stars around us hum.

Her warmth smells of clay and mica and quartz, and her voice tickles my soul once more.

< You are beautiful. You are desired— >

And I am loved. I smile.

ABOUT "THE LOSS OF LUNA"

Space fascinates me. It has since I was old enough to look up at the stars and wonder. Do planets feel lonely? What is their origin story? How many times have they fallen in and out of love in their long lives? My partner's company was invited to write bits and bobs about the moon for a time capsule that landed (in 2022) and for their contribution, they asked me to write a story. This is how "The Loss of Luna" came about.

HUNGRY

GET A CAT, they said. You work from home, it'll be great, they said. Besides, these days even an idiot can take care of a cat.

But I can't even take care of *me*!

They had a thousand and one reasons why I *needed* one and being the sucker I am, I caved. A cat owner I became.

What they hadn't *said* was how toddler-esque a cat would be, how utterly time-consuming said cat would be, or how being owned by a cat would result in picking up the ball, throwing the ball, and then pleading with the cat to *go get the damn ball*.

At least a dog would have fetched it.

Pantone peers at me over my laptop, his charcoal eyes unblinking in their silent plea, and I groan. Cat ownership might be new to me, but not *that* look; it's the same one my mother uses every time I stave off going home for the holidays.

When I flick his white-splotched rear, Pantone hops off my desk with a light chirp that his collar fails to interpret.

My stylus moves across the touch-screen, adding droplets of color to a website logo. The mock-ups are due to Garner Tech in three hours, but I still have two to go this afternoon.

Pantone meows, and the collar translates in a slightly flat digi-voice: I'M HUNGRY.

"You're always hungry, now shove off. It's not even four," I say, and Pantone cocks his head.

My email pings. Twice. I ignore it and continue working on the logo's capital G, whose curve is less semi-circle and more angular. Does Garner Tech want something smooth and soothing? Or harder--edgier...like a computer chip?

I'M HUNGRY.

An incoming call message pops up on my screen. Probably my roommate calling to gripe about being a sardine on the rail home. I flick it off-screen to the mailbox.

Pantone hops up on my desk, and I sigh, which he misreads as consent or approval.

I'M HUNGRY.

Red...is it too bloody looking? No one wants to associate a tech company with blood. Not after the latest child labor allegations. No, let's try something richer. Garnet maybe? Nope. Way too newb and cliché.

I'M HUNGRY.

"Enough, Pantone."

The garnet bleeds into the black outline too much for my tastes. "Undo," I say, and the mess is removed. Maybe green is a better idea. A tuft of orange fur and claws reach around my screen to bat at my stylus.

One black streak slashes the capital G. "UNDO," I growl. Pantone hooks the stylus's clip with a single claw and flings it at me where it bounces off my nose.

I'M HUNGRY.

"Dammit, cat, I'm busy!" I growl as he bats the stylus off my desk. All fifteen pounds of him follow it to the floor. A few trills and purrs follow as he rakes it with his rear legs. "Turn off *Cat-Speak* translations until 5 PM."

I'M--*purr, purr, chirrup.*

I fetch the stylus to a rumble of purrs and earn myself a scratch across three fingers. Just what I need. Maybe I'll contract cat scratch fever. Maybe red *will* work better than green...

WHEN THREE MINUTES of exposed belly doesn't elicit the desired belly-scritches, Pantone leaps onto my desk with a scolding chirp. He rubs his muzzle, half-white and half-orange, across the touch-screen's monitor like maybe *it* will feed him if he just rubs it hard enough. If I could afford the app, it would. I shake my head at the distraction. I literally can't afford it.

I touch my stylus to Pantone's muzzle to capture the color. There. A nice orangey-red for the logo. Perfect.

Pantone's vocalizations accelerate the closer it grows to five. The closer it grows to my deadline.

Why did I agree to take him in? Damn cat is nothing but an overly-large, expensive distraction.

The front door opens and closes in rapid succession. My peripheral vision confirms the presence of my roommate as I work on colorizing a sketch. As she enters the kitchen, she calls out, "Oooooo! Who's the admirer?"

I wave my stylus in her direction. "Garner sent 'em. I think they're hoping to woo me with flowers."

Joanie laughs. "Apparently they don't know about your black thumb. The last flora that arrived is still here. It's dead but has decided to pay rent. Speaking of rent...."

"I know, I know! It'll be there."

"It's due in two days. When is Garner paying you?"

I shrug. "Soon? They said I'd get paid for the mock-up designs almost immediately."

"Good. We got a note from the landlord. If we're late, we're out. I can't afford to lose this place." Joanie sets the lilies' vase on the dilapidated kitchen scanner. Its misaligned laser scans the vase, and the alarm sounds. I close my eyes at the flash of light, and wish I could close my ears as well.

WARNING: SCANNER IS IN NEED OF REPAIR. GARNER TECH IS NOT RESPONSIBLE FOR INJURY FROM MISUSE. PLEASE CALL A CERTIFIED TECH--

"Silence warning!" I shout from my living room desk. The sink's faucet releases a perfectly measured amount of water and tops off the vase.

"Thanks," Joanie says. "Any idea when the repairman is coming?"

I set aside my stylus, which Pantone stretches a paw toward. "When I get paid."

"So this Garner gig might be more than temporary freelance work? Something that pays like real work?"

I follow Joanie's gaze to Pantone, expecting my stylus to be a casualty on the floor, but it remains beside him as he watches me. The orange ring is but a sliver next to his wide pupils pooling with...it isn't hunger. No, something else. Sadness? Argh, cats don't get sad. They're just cats. Damn collar's turned off. No wonder I have no idea what he wants.

I shake my head and say, "Maybe. But not if I don't finish these designs."

Joanie mimes zipping her lips and sets the lilies on the counter. Pantone watches her retreat to the bathroom without comment.

She means well, but I grind my teeth at the reminder. Maybe we shouldn't have splurged on that pizza last week. I dangle the stylus over Pantone's head as a distraction. His eyes follow it a moment before he rests his head on his front paws. "That's what I get for trying to play with you. Figures."

He blinks at me slowly, something I've been told means he loves me, but I suspect he's only hungry.

"Moping won't get you fed any faster. It didn't get Puss-In-Boots fed any faster either, no matter what those old movies say."

Pantone closes his eyes.

I'M HALFWAY through the last design when Pantone leans his shoulder into my laptop and the screen tilts forty-five degrees. He sets his paw on its metal shell and shuts my laptop with a snap. The wall-clock chimes as he purrs. Five o'clock.

The LED light on his collar flips to green as *Cat-Speak 4.0* turns itself on. Pantone blinks slowly at me and opens his mouth.

I HURT.

"Dude, I know you're hungry--wait, what?"

Pantone stares at me but doesn't say anything else. "You hurt? Where?" I push my laptop aside to better reach him and run my hands across his back. No response. I gently massage his belly and hips as I've seen the vet do on television. Other than some squirming, nothing.

Is that good or bad? Has the collar malfunctioned?

I pull out the treat bag from my desk drawer. Rather than slink annoyingly around my ankles, he remains still, and when I toss two treats on the desk, he only sniffs them.

"You love tuna-treats," I say and shake the bag. He continues to stare at me.

I pop open my laptop. "Call Dr. Bruester."

The video call connects, and the regular receptionist is packing up her poodle-shaped purse. "Sunset Veterinary Clinic—this is Stacey. How may I help you, Melana?" She waves at Pantone as he drapes himself across my keyboard. His tail, which usually wags with trouble, lies still.

"Pantone's collar...well, it translated something a minute ago, and I'm really not sure what to do. Or if there's anything actually wrong...."

"What did Pantone say?" she asks.

"He said, 'I hurt.' Does he really? I mean, earlier he was just fine. What's wrong with him?"

Stacey frowns as she sets her purse on the counter. "Occasionally *Cat-Speak 4.0* will mix up expressions of contentment or enjoyment, but its pain sensors are very sophisticated. If he says he hurts, he's feeling pain. I would recommend you bring him in so Dr. Bruester can examine him."

I glance to the left of the call screen where a reminder flashes angry red letters at me. The designs are due in twenty minutes. No designs means no paycheck. No paycheck...well, that means no vet visit at a minimum. Probably no repairman. Not that it would matter if we were homeless.

She must have sensed my hesitation and says, "Dr. Bruester's about to leave, but if you bring Pantone into the clinic now, I'm sure he'd be willing to cut you an after-hours deal. It's probably nothing but better to be sure. Better to do what's best for Pantone."

But what about what's best for me? I have to eat, too.

Pantone meows. I HURT...A LOT.

Shit. Double shit. This is why I don't like pets. Pantone head butts me in the forehead, and I find myself saying, "We'll be there shortly."

Stacey ends the call as Pantone lets loose a raspy hurried purr. I HURT.

I give his head a careful pet before setting off in search of the cat carrier. Maybe Garner Tech really does use child labor. I'd be doing the world a favor by not giving them a flashy new logo.

My cat lies on his side, very still.

❦

PANTONE BURIES his head in the crook of my elbow. A brief knock announces Dr. Bruester's return, and Pantone trembles in my arms.

Two hundred dollars. The cost of a brief exam and blood draw. Another three hundred for a quick bio-scan. My doctor appointments are cheaper than my damn cat's.

Dr. Bruester's furrowed brows and squared shoulders make me regret this trip already. Something is wrong, and wrong usually spirals into expensive.

This is why I didn't want a pet to begin with. I can barely afford me.

The metal table between the doctor and me is littered with cat hair, which Dr. Bruester brushes off before taking a seat. He pops his tablet into its stand and swivels it so I can see. Numbers and squiggles scroll across its screen--not that they make any sense to me.

"Melana, has Pantone ingested anything unusual or odd in the last few hours?"

His question throws me, and I shuffle through the afternoon's memories. Pantone had complained he was hungry. I'd finished the second design. He'd complained again. I'd continued working. In fact, I'd had to mute his collar. Joanie had arrived home, and even muted, he'd continued to vocalize until four-ish.

Where'd he been at four? I frown. Had he been with me, or had he wandered off to another portion of the condo?

"Um, I'm not sure. He's been very vocal about his hunger all day. I had to silence the collar to get some work done...."

Dr. Bruester purses his lips into a tight circle. "Was there anything odd lying around the house he could have ingested? Any garlic left over from food preparation? New furniture?"

Pantone's damp paws leave furry prints across the examination table as he approaches the vet. I HURT.

"No," I say and shake my head. Pantone slinks back to me and head-butts me in the arm. "Nothing like that. I barely have the money in my account for this appointment, let alone new stuff. Why?"

"He's ingested something toxic. The blood work doesn't give me a clear picture of what, only that it's causing acute kidney failure. You said he was hungry, so I assume he's eaten something he shouldn't have. Though the scan didn't show any blockages. Any chance he got into a garbage compactor or garage?"

"The garbage compactor is emptied hourly, and Pantone's never left the condo. Our building doesn't even have a parking garage. The only plant I own died last--well, it died. I'm--I'm not good with living things." I glance at Pantone and frown. "It's why I got the collar. You know, so I could know what he needed."

Something tickles my brain, but Dr. Bruester interrupts when he asks, "What kind of plant was it?"

Pantone coughs, then vomits a mix of stomach acid and pink...*something*. "Is that chewing gum?" I ask as I point.

"Doubtful." Dr. Bruester scrapes some into a plastic dish. "I'll scan this in a moment and see what it is. Since money is an issue, we'll need to administer charcoal and get Pantone on IV fluids to flush the kidneys. He'll remain with us in the hospital for a day or two to see if the treatment takes. Of course, we'd be more successful if we knew what he got a hold of. Maybe look around your condo for clues."

My brain buzzes like the *Cat-Speak 4.0* collar when wet. "Dr. Bruester, how much is all of this going to cost? I mean, I want Pantone to be okay and all, but money's tight right now. I don't know if I can afford two days in the cat hospital."

He pets Pantone on the head as he levels his gaze on me. "I'll fetch the total for you, but I would highly encourage you to agree to the treatment. Without it, Pantone could die."

As if my now unfinished (*and unpaid for*) designs aren't sucker-punching me enough, Dr. Bruester's words claw their way into my gut where they duke it out with my guilt. If I had money, they'd just synthesize a new kidney or something, I'm sure. And if I'd fed Pantone earlier, maybe he wouldn't have gone searching for something else to eat. My first pet and of course I've fucked it up. He's gone and eaten--- *Oh god. The lily.*

"I think I figured it out!" I say, and Dr. Bruester pauses in his scan of the pink goo. "I landed a last minute design gig this week, and they sent me flowers. Well, lilies really. It was—" I glance at Pantone as he vomits up spittle and a wad of petal, "—pink. Are they bad for kitties? I didn't think he'd actually eat it."

"They're toxic to most cats and dogs. You'd be surprised at what cats will eat. We'll confirm the lily with our sample here to ensure he didn't ingest anything else."

"Does Pantone still need to be checked into the hospital?"

Dr. Bruester nods. "The treatment is mostly the same for a wide range of edible toxins." He turns off the scan-lens he wears and stares at me with his own green eyes. "I want you to understand—we'll do everything we can for Pantone, everything within your...budget—but we can't guarantee anything. Every animal reacts differently to toxins and poisons. We'll make him as comfortable as possible."

He points at the tablet. At the bottom of a long list is the total—a bright red number that equals my rent and then some. A lot of some.

If I did this, he might get better. Not that it would do him any good, because we'd probably be homeless. "Can you give me any odds? I mean, if I spend all this money and then he dies anyway, what's the point?" I ask.

Dr. Bruester nods, but his shoulders are slumped as he strokes Pantone's fur. "Usually by the time an animal reaches us, it's too late. They can't talk to us—" I raise an eyebrow at him, and he clears his throat. "—Yes, tech like the collar can help, but Pantone still can't tell you *when* he ate the lily. We can administer the charcoal and give him fluids, but after that, we wait. The decision of what to do is yours."

I glance down at Pantone. Sweet little hungry-goblin. Annoying hungry-goblin.

God, if I had tossed the lily—hell, if only I had never taken the Garner Tech job to begin with. How did people do this?

"If money is that tight, we could euthanize him. It might be more humane than kidney failure." His gaze could level an entire city block.

Bile burns the back of my throat. I can't afford this...but kill my cat? It's obvious what the doc thinks but....

Pantone's muscles quiver beneath my touch, but his purr is strong. I LOVE YOU.

My tongue sticks to the roof of my mouth, but I manage to choke out a few words. "I-I love you, too, little purr-bucket."

His purrs continue but don't translate.

And for the first time, I don't need them to.

A SPLATTER of sickly-yellow soup decorates my desk as I suck in instant-noodles. The box says chicken-flavored, but three cubes the size of tacks barely constitute "real" chicken. Pantone rolls his head in my direction and repeatedly sniffs the air. "No soup for you," I say as I dab the spillage with a napkin. "The last thing I need is another vet bill."

He swats at my napkin, his paw the only part of his leg with thick fur. I rub a finger over his shaved leg as my laptop wakes up. Purples and reds have faded to brown as the veins in his leg heal.

Another design job, another deadline, and an advance against another paycheck. At least this job has better ethics. I sip my soup as I pull up the design specs: a new logo for Sunset Veterinary Clinic.

I'M HUNGRY.

"Of course you are."

The former logo—a sun peeking out across a dog's head—reminds me of my grandmother's idea of the Internet: websites with garish colors that dance and lag via cable modem. The logo's sun bears both rings and rays, and the dog wears a space helmet from the 90's.

Space travel has come a long way since then, but this logo hasn't. Maybe if we update the helmet to the new face-fitting design....

I'M HUNGRY.

I scritch Pantone's ears and smile.

ABOUT "HUNGRY"

Originally published as a short e-book, "Hungry" was a story that came from an article in a veterinary medicine journal discussing the use of MRI's to translate basic needs in cats, be it hunger, pain, fear, etc. I was fascinated by the study and wondered what would happen if we could use the knowledge of their brain patterns to create the ever-talked-about talking collar, one that would allow us to know what our pets were thinking.

At least on a basic level.

The kicker being that if you could hear your cat (or pet) tell you that they love you, you could no more "put them down" or euthanize them than you could your child. Not easily anyway. So many pet owners see pets as disposable. Moving? Too bad, so sad for the puppy. So many vets and vet techs end up rescuing these healthy animals from euthanasia. They are living creatures. Sometimes helping them pass is needed, but it should be a difficult decision, not an easy one, which is why I wrote this story.

LIKE A HYPERCOLOR ACID-TRIP, our store's overhead florescent lights screamed their brightness at me, and I winced. A moment later, a sharp howl threatened to render my eardrums useless. The cry rose in pitch and warbled with every chin wobble as the toddler scrunched his eyes shut. Snot bubbled from his nose, and I shuddered.

Three days 'til Christmas meant every child within a twenty-mile radius ran screaming around my store. If they weren't capable of running, parents one cappuccino shy of a sugar coma carried them in, where they reached out with grubby hands to touch *everything*. These suckers were demanding, brutal, and *loud*. Five hours into my shift at Grab-a-Tabletop Games and my fake smile waned as cranky parents demanded out-of-stock games for half off retail.

Used to be one walked into their local game store to find the typical gamer ears deep in a campaign. Sure, they might have needed a shower and maybe fewer corn nuts, but the average age at the time was a solid twenty. With gaming's cool factor on a recent rise, tabletop became synonymous with "family-friendly." Meaning...*with* children. Whiny, spoiled, snot-nosed children who touched everything and left the store in need of a visit from the CDC.

The shrieking toddler toppled over on her butt, and I glanced around for the girl's attached parent. Two teens browsed the deck-builder section while some dude flipped through clearance bins. No one in particular hovered near the banshee. I picked up the phone to ping my boss when a woman in a 1-up t-shirt stepped out from behind the door marked "Employees only."

She spotted the crying toddler, and her lips curled in a snarl. "Why didn't you tell me she was crying?"

"Were you talking to me, ma'am?"

"Who else would I be talking to...uh, Megan?" she asked with a glance at my name tag.

"I'm sorry, ma'am. I couldn't find you when she began crying, but that door—that area's for employees only. Please do not go back there again." I tried to unobtrusively scan her pockets for mysterious bulges, and finding none, crossed my fingers she hadn't robbed us.

The older woman scooped up the toddler from the floor with a frown. "I had to pee. And don't call me ma'am, Megan. Makes me sound old." She bounced the toddler in her arms, changing the toddler's cries to hiccups.

My head pounded in a syncopated rhythm. Great. So she really *had* abandoned the child in my care. My skin crawled like a brush fire. Damn babies. I didn't like them, but I didn't usually find them so revolting. I curled my fingers into fists to keep from scratching my skin. Maybe it was the migraine.

The woman made a show of glancing through a few games, but the moment I turned away to ring up two teenaged shoppers, the woman slipped through the glass door, setting off another round of *Jingle Bell Rock* from the store's dancing Santa. Another gaggle of teens came in followed by a set of grandparents and a group of gamer bros, the latter of whom smirked when they met my gaze. A second rush of customers hit after explaining to the grandparents that a certain black-boxed party game wasn't an appropriate gift for a seven-year-old child.

One of the gamer bros glanced around the store in confusion for a good ten minutes before daring to step up to the register. My eyes attempted to crawl back behind their sockets at the brightness of his neon yellow shirt which declared him a "Rules Lawyer."

Oh goodie. My favorite type of customer. Noting his empty hands, I asked, "Sir, can I help you find something?"

"Um, well...I don't wanna be, um, rude, but dude, is there someone else here? I have a complicated question, ya know?"

Of course. *This* line of questioning. I sighed and slapped a bright, fake smile on my face. "I'm afraid I'm it, but I can help. Are you looking for something in particular?"

"Yeah, there's a new game deck out, but you wouldn't know anything about M—"

"Nisha vs. Odd Nicholas?"

Gamer bro froze, eyes wide. "Uh, yeah. But—"

"I'm sorry, but we're currently sold out. However, if you'd like to give me your info, we can call you if we get any more in before Christmas." Though I doubted it. That deck had been sold out since October's release.

"But—you're a girl. You play?"

I repressed the urge to educate him on the history of women in gaming. "I do. Is there anything else I can help you with?" I said instead.

He shook his head, brows still furrowed as he set off in search of his friends.

The rush continued to ebb and flow as the afternoon wore on. Ten minutes before closing, three children chased each other in circles around the store while a foul stench wafted up from a nearby stroller. It was the stuff of nightmares—a mix of sweet and sour that had nothing to do with Chinese food and everything to do with a baby's explosive diarrhea.

"Do you have a restroom?" the mother asked as she rocked the stroller back and forth.

As if that would help the disaster that awaited her in that diaper.

I opened my mouth to reply in the negative, but the way her eyes pleaded with me, the way the baby's face screwed up in preparation for one hell-of-a-shriek, I couldn't refuse. I ushered her through the door marked 'Employees Only' and returned to checking out the flood of last minute customers that had come crashing into the store in my sudden absence.

My cell phone read ten minutes past closing by the time the last customer was gone. After clearing the demo-tables and display cases of fingerprints and germs-a-plenty, I pushed a mop cart down the hall towards the employee bathroom. When I cracked the door open, a rotten smell wafted into my nose, and I dry-heaved.

Shit was everywhere. Literally.

From the sides of the toilet to the sink that had probably been used as a changing station, excrement colored the bathroom with a green that clashed against the room's orange tile. It was something out of a nightmare—my nightmare in fact—and as I stood there on my Saturday night, I gave great consideration to quitting. But I'd worked for the Terrys for nine years. They were family friends, and besides, gaming was my world—my usually child-free world—but my world nonetheless.

The one day the boss man calls in sick, and we get explosive babies. No wonder he never let anyone use the restroom. At this rate, it'd be ages before the bathroom would be clean.

Donning yellow rubber gloves clear up to my elbows, a bottle of bleach, and my pounding migraine, I dived headlong into scrubbing the sink, then worked my way down to the floor. Bits of poo resisted me as they burrowed their way into cracked grout, and I sighed. No way was I going to let somebody's baby permanently scent-mark a place I used daily. I scoured the floor between gags. Previous migraines had heightened my sense of smell before, causing nausea and vomiting, but nothing like this. The sharpness of bleach and sweetness of baby poop wound its way up my nose until desperation drove me to donning a face mask.

By the time I'd finished, bright white grout and orange tile shined back at me ever-too-brightly. I tossed most of the cleaning supplies in a trash bag and stumbled my way outside. After locking the door behind me, I threw the smelly bag in the lot's dumpster and fell into my car seat with a wince.

The gray season was upon us, a fact for which I was grateful. The last thing my migraine needed was a stare-off with a blazing ball of fire in the sky. A light misting of rain decorated my windshield enough to warrant wipers, and my brain throbbed in rhythm to them as they squeaked their way across the glass on my drive home.

Or at least, home was where I'd intended to drive.

I leaned my head against the steering wheel to avoid staring at a glaring red light. What I thought was a light honk startled me, and when

I opened my eyes, a customer stood in front of me, her grimace all too familiar.

"Welcome back from dreamland. You gonna ring me up, or am I gonna be standing here 'til Christmas?" The woman slapped a board game box on the counter.

"Wait...what? How'd I—"

The woman's right eye twitched as she glared at me. "I *sa-id*—" She stretched out the word like it would somehow answer my confusion. "Are you gonna ring me up? Before Christmas?"

"I-I thought I was driving home. How'd I get here?" I asked, and when her scowl deepened, I waved a hand in her direction. "Never mind. I'm sorry, ma'am. Let me get this for you."

Her game was paid for and bagged in moments, though her expression never changed. Once the dancing Santa announced her exit, I sneaked a look at my phone.

1: 22 PM. December 24th.

Somewhere, I'd lost my entire evening and then some. When had I gotten home? What had I done last night? And how'd I get back at work already? I shook my head. That must've been one hell of a migraine!

Another customer approached the counter, this one coughing hard enough to dislodge a lung, followed by another customer with a gaggle of children who yammered nonstop about their lengthy list of demands for Santa. When a third customer asked to use the restroom, I replied with a firm *no* as images from yesterday's fiasco flashed through my mind.

I glanced at my phone. *5:43 PM.* Long past closing time for Christmas Eve.

What the actual fuck? Four customers didn't amount to four hours' time.

The *OPEN* sign's purple neon fizzled once before flickering to black. The lone customer in the shop glanced at something over my shoulder and grinned, his mouth too wide and lips too thin as they stretched grotesquely across too pale a face. A sudden weight on my shoulder announced the hand before four fingers squeezed my collar bone, and I let loose a scream that cracked as the neon light flared to life before fizzling out. I spun to find no one behind me, and when I touched my shoulder, nothing was there.

The weight was gone.

The store now stood empty and dark as half the lights were off, just like the neon sign. When I blinked and suddenly found myself in my bed rather than the game store, I sighed in relief. I was dreaming. That's what it all had been.

One horrendous, child-filled nightmare.

No one had grabbed me, no one had teleported me, and I certainly hadn't lost any time. My head didn't pound anymore either. The holiday season had been particularly brutal and as a result, I'd been dreaming the day from hell. Mystery behind me, I closed my eyes and slept.

Or more like drifted through a retail-land flooded with angry customers and screaming toddlers. Despite this, my consciousness knew I dreamed enough to be irritated by the topics plaguing my subconscious. Next thing, my mother would make a guest appearance to complain about her lack of grandchildren.

Something made a noise outside the bedroom.

I couldn't quite tell what it was, but the sound of something falling over reached me even in sleep. The hair on my arms stood up as my brain fought to process what it had heard.

Had it been something tipping over on the bookcase in the hall, or had it been someone brushing against the trash can in the kitchen? Or were the sounds nothing more than my dreaming? When nothing more happened, my eyelids closed heavier over my eyes and my breathing slowed.

Moments before I'd found deep sleep, the *thud* of something hard knocking the corner of my dresser pulled me away from another horrible customer who screamed at me in my head. That had been *too* real.

Footsteps sounded near my bed, but I kept my eyelids clamped tightly in place. If I opened them, I'd have to admit that someone was somehow in my house. In spite of my alarm system being on—I *had* set it, right? Yes. Via app before crawling into bed, or so my foggy mind told me—someone stood to my left. Their shallow breath sprinkled fumes of garlic and mint across my nostrils, and I ground my teeth to silence my screaming.

Unable to stop myself, I pulled my left hand from under the comforter and lifted it in the air. Eyes closed, I fumbled around until my hand found the face of whoever knelt at my bedside. My fingers crawled across cold skin until they found a mouth.

An open mouth.

I reached inside to feel jagged incisors that spoke of missed dental visits, followed by sharp canines, then the familiar bumps of well-ground molars. The tongue dripped with sticky saliva, and I gagged.

If I smelled my fingers, would they reek of garlic? Or mint?

The open mouth let loose a hot scream that didn't stop, and I tugged my hand away too late. A tingling sensation brushed across my fingers a split second before brute pain throbbed as lava-like blood flowed into one side of the mouth.

I couldn't help it. I had to see.

The scream became a wild and panicked pant, and when I opened my eyes, I stood behind the counter of Grab a Table Top Games, a long line of children crying and pleading and begging. For games, for chocolate, for soda, and for anything we didn't sell.

My fingers were stuffed into my mouth where they muffled the shrieks coming from me. The metallic taste of blood pooled in the crevices of my teeth, and when I pulled my fingers from my mouth, they came away bloody.

I'd bitten off my fingertips.

The mouth had been my own.

ABOUT "MOUTH"

As someone who's worked retail during the holidays, the stories of what people are capable of still haunts me. "Mouth" is a bit of a psychological horror story that came to me in one sitting. Sometimes the stories happen like that. It's creepy in all the ways that people can identify with, especially if they have anxiety and have worked retail. Retail is a special sort of hell.

ONLY A BIRD

TODAY WAS SUPPOSED to be good, to be amazing. In fact, it was destined to be a good day because it was Friday, and every Friday, the factories let loose their newest animal automata to test whether or not they worked. A strong gust of wind might display a weakness in a bird's wing-strength, or a dog might run out into rush-hour traffic only to end up a pile of chips and bolts, manufactured-sinew, and unlit eye-sockets. Whatever they tested, most of the city paused on a Friday. As a whole, we took a deep breath in the afternoon, and today should have been no exception.

Today was supposed to be simple.

Besides being automata test day, it was also the first week of school, and I'd had everything ready five days prior. The summer's dust covers had been packed away in classroom cabinets while the hiss of the air conditioner cycled stale air. Computer stations had been thoroughly updated, eBooks and tutorial programs pre-loaded and waiting for 140 sleepy heads to walk through my computer lab's doors. By Thursday, my routine moved like a well-oiled test-engine.

First, welcome the students as they walked into class. The doorway scanned their ID for attendance and once the bell rang, it was time to teach the lesson. Observe as students practiced at their stations, answer questions, and finally, chat with students on their way out of class before starting the cycle all over again. Times seven.

But this was Friday—all I had to do was wake up, get ready for the day, sit in my car as it navigated through traffic, and once at work, give a test. No new instruction. No worrying about bandwidth or whether new logins would work. On test days, I was little more than a glorified babysitter. That's why I get paid the big bucks.

11:45 AM CST. That's when shit hit the proverbial fan.

As my own feet trudged towards the traditional brick school building—thoughts rushing ahead toward the weekend—three pair in leather pounded pavement to reach me. One pair of hands, palms up, stretched out to me. A golden fluff was contained all too tightly by sweaty fingers—a fledgling yellow finch.

Their words were hurried and fast.

"We found it on the ground under a nest!"

"We threw it up so it would fly, but it slammed into the brick wall."

"It couldn't fly, and we don't know what to do."

Verbiage in triplet slammed against my wall of calm. Quick examination showed no visible sign of injury—just one bird breathing a mile a minute in panic as it failed to escape its captors. I couldn't see any visible gears or tech, but that didn't mean anything. Automata or real, the bird was panicking.

I ushered the three six graders into the building and then my lab where a terrified feather-head was bundled gently into a small box. Water was given via drops from my fingertips. Students, fearing they'd injured it further, refused to leave the bird's sun-vibrant side. Calm ensued for a brief, yet subtle moment as the bird burrowed into safety. Security.

A chiming electronic bell meant the beginning of class and as the three students reluctantly parted, twenty more entered the lab, quietly wondering at the chaos as they met a closed door and no teacher greeting them.

Before 9:00:00 AM, every child in the building knew about the bird, and every staff member as well. Even the principal found reason to make an appearance in the lab and see what creature was being cared for this semester. Last year, it had been a baby duck, abandoned by its mother on the day of the state mandated testing. A wildlife rehabilitator was called and said duck had been saved.

To my school, I'm more than a computer teacher. I'm the "veterinarian-in-residence" as I'd been pre-vet in college before changing majors. Or maybe it's because I give a shit about animals. Even automata. If something is found injured, it's brought to me. No matter the animal, I was willing to give it a go as all life is sacred to me, down to the last ant.

There would be no test today in this class period as the bird made for a unique life lesson. A teachable moment they say in the teaching field. Words spoken at barely a whisper as twenty bodies huddled in a fascinated circle.

"What happened to it?"

"Where'd you get it?"

"Is it really an it? I mean, it's got to be a boy or a girl, right?"

"Is it a test bird? Or is it real? I've never felt feathers so soft before!"

While my mouth was a revolving door of answers, my classroom was a circus of stillness as quiet people entered and exited, each one a visitor to put vision to the rumors heard in halls. Fascinated science teacher. Worried reading teacher and pet owner. Each one "oooooh"ing over the tiny life held so fragile by black and white threads in cardboard.

By second period, a rehabilitator was found, but transportation was an issue. The sun would be high in the sky before a hero could arrive and thus the wait began—a frantic wait as the clock ticked and spelled doom for the fledgling. No teacher was willing to watch my class, so that I could drive the bird to its savior. I tried and failed to reach someone at the factories. Of course.

If their test subjects died, data would reach them one way or another. Why would anyone in the public need to reach them personally?

Despite staff concern, their sympathy was very limited and did not include any real desire to help. After all, it was "only a bird." Time passed like a slug over cobble and the bird slept, huddled against a QWERTY sporting blanket, olive wings tucked against a warm belly—a breathing golden belly. I checked my email—maybe someone would step up.

"I heard you have a bird. Can I feed it to the class snake if it takes a turn for the worse?"

"Quail for dinner anyone? LOL!"

"It's a bird. Need me to put it out of its misery? HAHA!"

Coworkers' "concern" lay before me in text that blurred, both in rage and in sorrow. Just the idea that an adult, with the supposed maturity level of one full-grown, could joke about such a thing when a helpless being's life hung in the balance disturbed me. The cavalier attitude with which they joked about life and death set my teeth on edge. I was a known animal-lover and caregiver, and they found it *funny*. Harsh words from cold-hearted people who were tasked with developing impressionable minds. If it was so easy not to care about "only a bird," how easy would it be to write off a thirteen-year-old child? I sucked in a slow breath to calm myself and exhaled through a grimace.

10:05 AM. 10:09 AM. 10:15 AM. Another bell ring. Another set of anxious students trying oh-so-hard not to push as they held their breath. Little ones afraid to alarm the bird. Afraid to hurt the injured patient in the corner of the room. Like an elephant, it weighed on them as they chose their answers on a test on which none of them could focus. Honestly, neither could I. Eyes pass over the clock again. Waiting. Waiting for a saint to arrive and save "only a bird."

"Can we see the bird?"

"Please?"

"We'll be quiet."

Whispers in unison echo through the still air. A nod and twenty-two bodies creep towards the box. For the first time since that morning, my hands gently cupped the box and lifted it from the nearby chair. Forty-four ovals of green, blue, brown, and mixes in between stare.

As if it wished to entertain my kiddos, the bird rose up from the blanket, olive wings spread wide as his eyes opened fully. Two wing beats and his body shook suddenly, a sharp popping sound from within, and he fell. His limp body collapsed on a cushion of white, his head swinging upside down as if an invisible hand had snapped the twig-like neck.

For a moment, nothing. Silence. Emptiness. Then cries.

"What happened?"

"Oh God. Did it die?"

"Fix it. Please?"

Nothing prepares you for that moment—the time when you must explain life and death to the heart and mind of a child. Challenging enough to explain it to myself as I stared, horrified, at the body in my hands. What had first been a temporary home, a shelter, was now his softly lined casket.

"He's dead." Such a sense of finality to the words. Was it sending data across invisible air waves to its maker? Or was a ghostly bird flying away to wherever dead animals go?

When a student commented, "Wouldn't it be cool if he just rose up and flew away? Like 'Gotcha!'" it served only as permission for the waterworks to begin. Twelve year old boys trying oh-so-hard to be a 'man' looked anywhere but towards the slowly stiffening little bird.

Girls huddled together, open weeping, some even praying. It was an odd scene as grief swept over us. All of this over something that was "only a bird." One special child, autistic in nature, reached out a darkened hand to touch the feathers of a once warm creature and stroked it gently, as if the bird would break yet again.

The bird didn't move. No notice was given to the motion, nor the care that went with it. Whatever had been, was no longer present.

"His eyes are still open."

And then my little autistic boy crumbled like sand. Somehow, through the fog of his mind, he knew this was death. It was final. Forever. The End. And it ate at him like a cancer. A counselor was dialed and soon we were one student shy of our twenty-two bodies.

"Can we bury him?"

"He needs a funeral."

"First, he needs a name."

Sincerity from the mouths of babes. No one asked if it was a real bird. No one cared. One moment it had been alive and the next it wasn't. In that moment, we had lost something profound. An innocence maybe.

It wasn't coworkers who helped me cope with the loss of this tiny being, but the children around me who held my hand as we ventured forth into the Texas heat. No one complained about the hot sun on our backs as a cold had enveloped us. The bird's head flopped back and forth with each heavy step towards the earth. We picked a shaded spot under the tree where his nest, his home, had been and forty-four hands *(mine included)* set to scooping dirt from below their feet.

The box went in, blanket and all, wrapping the petite body in the warmth of our caring. Dirt sprayed across him—no longer a bird, just a body—and covered first him, then the sides of the box until only a small mound was left.

"His name is Mustard—He just looks like a Mustard."

Delicate laugh, then acceptance.

"We need flowers."

"And a grave marker. And...some words?"

Several girls grabbed flowers from a nearby begonia as another gathered a few twigs from the ground. A hasty cross, lopsided and ill-formed stood before the mound and flowers laid carefully nearby.

I said nothing. What words could ease their heavy hearts? While I grappled with my seemingly misfunctioning brain for the right words, or hell, any words for that matter, our autistic classmate rested a hand on my shoulder. I hadn't seen him return, let alone heard him come through the squeaking doors out back.

His eyes met mine then, still pink and wet with tears unshed, but he carried a confidence with him that spoke. *I got this,* they said. At my nod, his voice cut through the crying.

"It's better that he isn't suffering anymore. He died like I'd want— surrounded by people who care about me."

Wisdom that had failed me in my own sorrow and with it, permission to move past the event. Our legs carried us back to class where they shared stories of lost pets. Lost friends. Lost family members. Sharing made the grief easier to bear.

Somehow, I'd have to find the words to tell the rest of the students of the bird's tragic death, but the task somehow felt easier now.

If my students could be moved over "only a bird," then there was hope yet for the world. Maybe the world wasn't destined to be full of snarky, callous people who felt nothing, who dreamed only for themselves. Even though the eyes of my coworkers held humor as they gazed into my naked pain, it didn't matter.

Truly alive or mechanical, that little bird had lived more dead then their desensitized hearts ever could.

ABOUT "ONLY A BIRD"

The bird in this story may be automata *(or maybe not)*, but the story of "Only a Bird" is real and pulled directly from my years as a public school teacher. The messages in this from my former coworkers are real as well. Never have I worked with such a group of cold-hearted people in my entire life. That school was full of them, and sadly, most went on to be administrators. No wonder most kids hate school.

OH MY GOD.

It was a blank screen. The *most* intimidating visual ever the night before a paper was due to Professor Snap-Pants. *(If I took the time to explain the nickname, we'd be here all night and I'd be no closer to finishing this damn paper on economics during the civil war. Hey—the topic sounded good when I thought of it yesterday morning!)* Either way, I was screwed.

Another C would render my financial aid as useless as butter is to a cat. Speaking of that, did you see the video posted yesterday on YouTube? The one with the cat grooming a stick of butter? I swear I breathed soda... ugh, the paper. Okay, I could do this. I could.

The cursor blinked at me.

Financial aid wasn't my only concern. I could already hear my granny lecturing me on the importance of a college education. "I ain't seen none a college classroom. If that state might could pay your way, you gonna go if I gotta knock a hole in someone's head."

I *had* to pass this class.

Earlier that afternoon, my grade had tumbled as low as my self-esteem. After yet another lecture on how the economy drove the pricing of everything, including that of tuition and books, Professor Snap-Pants had passed back our tests. He had literally held my future in his hands.

My fellow freshmen had ignored the man's love for striped

polyester that swished as he paced, ignored his gravelly voice as he lectured us about the importance of studying, and lastly, had avoided his gaze as they tweeted and texted their way through the tail-end of class.

His lectures were always the same—our understanding of this economy could "change the world!" Like anything I ever did was gonna change something as big as the world.

My empty fingers had danced across my used textbook—its dog-eared pages and random highlighter marks screaming my poverty to a sea of white that had bought their textbooks brand-spankin'-new. What could this man know of tuition? He might wear a 'stache that screamed failed '80s TV actor, but he drove a Porche. I'd sighed loud enough for his TA to glance my way.

My butt had stuck to the chair, sweat sticking me in place.

Professor Snap-Pants had laid my paper across my desk. "I expected better than this from you."

I'd almost vomited when he'd said it. It didn't matter whether he'd meant "from a scholarship student" or "from a woman of color." When I'd turned the test over, the numbers swam before settling into a big 7-0. Seventy. Passing by one point.

For once, I had been glad my phone was dead. If I'd had a text message alerting me to posted grades, I'd have decorated the room all sorts of colors. "Professor?"

He'd stopped at the door but didn't face me.

"I—I was wondering... if there was any extra credit I could do. I know my grade sucks—"

"I don't normally offer extra credit for an introductory course. However, I may have something to help. Let me think on it and get back to you. I'll send a message through campus text." And with that, he'd left me alone in the classroom.

A few hours later, I still needed a new phone.

And a new brain.

And the cursor was still blinking at me. Dammit.

A knock saved me from another five minutes of cold, one-dimensional staring. My girlfriend, Alyce, whose frame easily stretched the height of the dormitory door, smirked as she entered. She held a wrapped package in both hands. "Mikala, I've been texting you for the past hour!"

I pointed to the plastic container beside me where my phone swam in a sea of rice.

"Oh, right. Have you powered it on yet?" The *do-I-look-stupid* face I made didn't fool her. "You did, didn't you?"

I flicked a pellet of rice at the wall. "I did, and it's dead. Officially fried crispy. Oh god," I muttered with a glance at the computer screen. "How did it get to be after five already?"

Alyce tossed the box onto my bed and closed the door behind her. "You owe me, Mikala."

"For what?"

"Retrieving your package from Basement Giant. Resident Assistant or not, he gives me the creeps. How can you stand him in class?"

My knees knocked the bed frame as I fetched the box. A muttered curse or three later, I rubbed my fingers across the smooth label. Water droplets morphed the writing and sent my far-sightedness into a shit fit. "What the hell does this even say? Are you sure it's mine?"

"Basement Giant—"

"His name's Greg," I muttered, but she rambled on without hearing me.

"—said it was for you. You gonna open it? Maybe it's a *luuuuurve* letter. Didn't you tell him you're already taken?"

My cheeks grew warm—not that she'd notice—the blessing and the curse of dark skin. Alyce plopped onto the bed, and I scooched away from my girlfriend's mess of elbows and knees arranging themselves into some weird mix of yoga and sitting. "Letters come in an envelope," I said. The wrapping paper was taped too neat to be from Baseme—Greg —and I said as much.

"Still say it's from Basement Giant. You know he's all set to get some booty now that your exotic self has blessed his dormitory." When I rolled my eyes, she added, "Honey, you know boys. They get all hot and bothered at the thought of gay women. As if our sole purpose is to provide eye candy or a threesome. I should write a paper about that. Certainly a better topic than"—she glanced at my computer screen— "'The Civil War's Impact on the Economics of the United States.' How can you stand that class?" Without waiting for an answer, she tapped the box and said, "You act like it's drugs or something. Open it already."

I don't know why I cared about preserving the paper. Maybe it was my granny rubbing off on me. She didn't waste a thing. Never knew when money would be tight again, and you'd find yourself needing whatever it was you'd tossed.

The tape peeled up by the edges without tearing the brown paper, which fell away to reveal a white box bearing a single smiley face. My stomach sucker-punched my esophagus.

"What's in the *box*? What's in the *box*?" Alyce cried as she wrung her hands in an overly dramatic fashion.

Leave it to her to quote Greg's favorite movie. I only knew *that* because he played it on repeat in his room every evening. Not that I'd been anywhere near that dank basement he called a dorm room—just that you could hear it bleeding into the laundry room. I popped the top open and frowned.

"Peanuts. Lucky you!"

I slapped Alyce's hand away as she snatched a foam peanut. One handful at a time, I dumped them into the small recycling can beside my bed until my fingers brushed the bottom.

"No way." I pulled out the plastic clamshell wrapping—a hell only second to my paper—and held it up. "You said this was *from* Greg?"

Her mouth formed a silent O.

"As in, he sent this to me? Or was it in the mailroom, and he was going through the mail?" I asked.

"Um, he said it was for you, Mikala. I assumed it was from him, but I guess he coulda snagged it from the mailman or something. What kind is it? Lemme see."

Damn clamshell was closed tighter than Greg's lips at a frat party. I twisted the plastic, and a line of blood appeared across my index finger.

Now the damn thing possessed teeth.

Alyce waved a hand at me. "Give me that thing before you kill someone with it. Oooooh! It's the new Micro-Lunia III!" She made clean cuts all along the clamshell's four sides with scissors borrowed from my desk. The phone tumbled from its prison.

Everything spilled across the bed—plastic, instruction manual, and shiny new phone. "I would've peeled down the top myself," I said as she caught the phone. All $900 overpriced dollars of it.

Her blue eyes twinkled in response. "I bet you would've

"Kinda creepy, but how'd Greg know I needed a replacement?" I asked.

"Probably overheard me mention it in the hall." She set the phone in my waiting hand.

I'd expected cold stainless steel, not plastic. When my thumb brushed the screen, the blue glow displayed a happily bouncing cube. *(How else would you describe an animated cube wearing a grin as it tap danced like Fred Astaire? Way too freakin' happy for my tastes.)* My finger hesitated, and the happy cube waved at me. I dropped the phone.

"What the hell? You looking to kill another phone?" asked Alyce as she pointed at the phone lying face down on the carpet.

"Damn thing waved at me."

"It waved?" Alyce bent over to retrieve the phone, whose screen was now black. "Um, I think you broke it, Mikala."

"Good. I don't want some freakishly happy phone."

My fingers trembled as I retrieved an escapee peanut from the floor. I tossed it and the phone's plastic in the recycling can. It wasn't like I'd never seen animation before—my bank's damn ATM used animation to capture the user's attention—but something about the dancing cube unnerved me.

I fetched the phone and tossed it in the can. Alyce winced but said nothing. "Alyce, I'm afraid you'll have to hit the party on the third floor yourself. I'll catch up, assuming I finish this freaking essay."

She unfolded herself from the bed in one smooth motion. "Okay, but if you don't make it there by midnight, I'm sending up a search party."

"As long as they come phoneless," I said.

Her laughter followed her out the door, which I kicked shut from my chair.

The blank page waited patiently.

10 P.M. REARED its ugly head with all the bells and whistles of snorting myself awake. For the third time.

If *I* couldn't stay awake writing this essay, what would happen to Professor Snap-Pants when he graded it? Damn fool would likely sleep himself into a coma at this rate. I rubbed my eyes and took another swallow of Grapetastic-Flex. Energy drinks were for losers and freshmen like me.

I stared at the bottle's bottom rim, where a teaspoon of purple liquid remained. When had I drunk the rest?

The bottle was tossed into the recycling can where it bounced off something—something that trilled and tweeted. Then that something chirped, followed by a long buzz. Bright blue light reflected off the empty bottle, sending tiny star-lights dancing around the metal bin.

"Fine. Let's see you wiggle, you stupid thing," I muttered as I fished out the phone.

I'd seen something like this before—back in the days when software companies thought cute animations would prevent users from wishing they'd die in a fire. It reminded me of Clipsy, and I scowled.

The cube—whatever it was called—waved at me. I flipped the bird at the phone, but he continued his tap dance. Huh. I touched my thumb to the screen, and my thumbprint flashed once before dissolving. The home screen looked just like my deceased phone, right down to the dancing kitten icon for YouTube. Maybe just one video...

But when I single-tapped the icon, a warning screen popped up.

INTERNET DISABLED—Distraction-Free App Enabled.

What the hell was this? I scrolled past two screens of apps until I found the Settings icon. Nestled in the privacy controls lay the offending app. I flipped the tab to disabled. Another pop-up.

ARE YOU SURE? Y/N

I jabbed the 'Y' and closed out of Settings.

Thirty seconds later, a video of an everyday hero saving a drowning cat filled the phone's screen. Just as he leaped off the bridge into the icy water below, a pop-up appeared.

IS THERE SOMETHING ELSE YOU SHOULD BE DOING? Y/N

"What. The. Hell." I slammed the phone on my desk. The message disappeared only to be replaced by the dancing cube. "Okay, that's it. How do I uninstall this shit?"

I slid my finger across the screen, but the cube held up a one-fingered hand. A dialogue box appeared next to him. "Need help with a paper? Let Q-Be help!"

Oh my god. It really was some new evolution of Clipsy! I smirked at his silly dance, but when he gestured for me to click, what can I say? I was curious, and it *was* after 10. I walked through a series of questions about my topic, education level, even writers I admired, and by 10:20 p.m., Q-Be spit out a list of links as long as my braids and from primary sources, no less! I clicked the first link and a sea of text scrolled across my phone's screen. The first book had to have been written during the Civil War. No one sounded *that* southern anymore. 'Cept maybe my granny.

My vision glazed over as I scanned paragraph after paragraph. Did it really matter that some economist felt our current economic woes stemmed from war? Yet another blowhard bitching that his southern pride meant more than the freedom of fellow human beings. Professor Snap-Pants had a particular hard-on for those that argued the Civil War caused irreparable harm to the South's cotton production. As the "token black person" in class—hell, in the economics department even —who was I to argue the point alone?

Pick my battles and all that. This class, this professor—wasn't one of them. Besides, with my luck I'd be the wrong kind of statistic if I ruffled feathers in good ol' northern Florida.

My head throbbed, and my eyes were too dry to see straight. Q-Be danced across the screen in a wavy blur. "Need help? How about a tutor?"

I clicked through a few privacy notices and TOS screens before Q-Be danced away. Ten seconds later, my phone lit up with a genuine text message.

Hey, Mikala. Still needing help on that paper?

Who's this? I typed back.

Q-Be said you needed a tutor for your Econ 101 paper.

Yeah, I do. But who's this? How do I know you aren't some online freakazoid? Have you even taken economics?

Three dots appeared as the person typed a rather lengthy response. Then they disappeared before a short reply. *Econ major. Need help?*

An honest-to-god economics major?! No way!

"Thank you, Q-Be," I whispered. I stopped just short of kissing the phone. Had to draw a line somewhere.

How does this work? Do we meet? Work online? Are you even local to Tallahassee?

Even better. I'm in your dorm.

Goosebumps spread across my bare arms. Creepy turned scary. I typed a curt reply. *How do you know who and where I am? Are you STALKING me?*

No, just another student. A friend of a friend, you could say. Figured you needed help.

I should've texted Alyce. She'd set the creeper straight.

Q-Be poked his head around the text message screen's corner and waved. "All of our tutors are screened using a rigorous process that includes a background check, fingerprinting, and drug screening. Your safety is our priority, so you continue to Q-Be!" he said by way of green dialogue box.

The econ major was probably safe enough, but I couldn't shake the rolling nausea in my stomach. I texted back, *Either you level with me, or I'll drop this phone down a garbage disposal.*

Three more dots as Q-Be wiggled his square butt in the screen's bottom right corner.

I heard Alyce talking about your grades in the mailroom. You know how much of a gossip she is. I'm harmless, I swear.

Fine. Where do we meet?

My dorm room's pretty big. I don't have a roommate. Lots of comfy chairs.

Like hell. Comfortable chairs or not, that was a surefire way to get dead. I texted back, *Um, how 'bout the common study, 2nd floor.*

See you in 5.

I stood in front of my dorm's closed door for three of those five minutes, my legs less human and more octopus. Q-Be buzzed a reminder and with a deep sigh, I took control of my wobbly legs and left my dorm.

Alyce would kill me when she found out.

TEN-FIFTY P.M. the night before a major paper was due, and I honestly figured the dorm's study would be the hoppin' place. Instead of dozens of sleepy heads bowed over books, two students curled up in the comfy beanbag chairs near the rear, one with her headphones blasting some J-pop piece while she messed with her cell. The other—-my tutor I guessed—-sat with his back to me, his hoodie pulled up over his head.

I spied a beat-up, dog-eared copy of *Economics for Dum-Dums* peeking out from under his elbow, and my face grew hot as I approached. "I thought you said you were an econ major!"

Greg looked up from a notebook full of scribbles. "I am."

I told you so! mocked Alyce's voice in my head. My "tutor" was Greg, and I resisted the urge to flip Q-Be the bird.

"What's with the Dum-Dums book?"

The gray hoodie hid most of his orange curls, but a few peeked out when he glanced down. "I thought it... might be well, you know... easier for you?"

"This isn't gonna work—"

"Wait," he called out as I turned away. "You need help, right? No one knows Professor Frederick's class the way I do. You know that."

"I do?"

"Do you even pay attention in class?" He held up the notebook of scribbles. "I've been his TA for the past two years. I handed out some of the test papers today right in front of you."

If he stood up, I guessed he looked tall enough to be the lumbering shape that hovered in the classroom corner while Professor Snap-Pants lectured. I'd never given the figure much notice. "So if you're the TA, why haven't you taught a class? Isn't that what TAs are supposed to do or something?"

"Professor Frederick takes the semester's first half, while it's still cool outside. Closer we get to spring, the more I'll take over." When I cocked an eyebrow, he added, "He likes to hit the beach."

I snorted. "Professor Snap-Pants... at the beach? Does he tan his ankles or does the man actually own something other than those hideous running pants?"

"Snap-Pants? Is that... what the students... call him?" he asked between laughs. "I'll never see him the same way again. Look what you've done!"

The girl wearing headphones glared at us as she fled Greg's braying chuckles. She snapped a pic from the doorway, and I groaned. Great. Now we'd be up on social media... together. Alyce would kill me for hanging with creepy Greg.

I snagged a chair across the table from Greg. Q-Be was gloriously silent as we worked—Greg teaching from a book, his notes, or some app on his phone as I pecked away on my laptop's keyboard.

When Greg taught, the creepy mailbox stalker image faded and left behind a normal, polite TA. So normal, it was easy to lose track of time. Midnight came and went. By the very early morning hours, my paper was done.

By the time I dragged my laptop up to my dorm room, I'd forgotten all about Alyce's rescue party. I unlocked the door expecting a dark room and instead found blaring lights and our friend, Sam, lounging on my bed.

She dropped her book when she saw me. "Oh-my-god-where-have-you-been? Hold-up-don't-answer-I-need-to-call-Alyce—" Her fingers danced across her phone as she took a breath. "Alyce-I-found-her-she's-here... okay... I will." Sam shoved her phone into her hip pocket.

"Alyce's on her way. She says *stay here.*"

I frowned. "O-kay. I wasn't aware I was missing."

Sam shot me a look that clearly said otherwise before scooting out the door. My phone pulsed. When I slid my thumb across it, Q-Be waved.

DO YOU NEED HELP WITH A MISSING PERSON? Y/N

I was still laughing when Alyce barged through the door to our dorm room. A few locks had escaped her lopsided bun, and she jabbed me in the collarbone. "Where have you been?"

"In the study. Why?"

Her wide eyes tightened as she claimed the rolly chair. "You didn't come to the party."

"I had to finish my paper. Look, I'm sorry that I worried you, but I had to finish the damn thing."

"When you didn't show, I sent Sam to get you—"

Now I remembered. "The search party... oops."

"Yeah. Sam called and said you weren't answering, and I thought something was wrong." My phone bleeped, and Alyce frowned. "I thought you threw that thing away? Anyway, when I got here, your laptop was gone. Didn't know what to think."

I smiled as Q-Be did a back flip. "What can I say? He grew on me."

"He? He who?"

I opened my mouth, fully intending to say Q-Be, but the G tumbled from my brain to my lips without warning. "Gr—" My hand muffled the offending word, and Alyce snatched the phone from my fingers.

"You didn't!" she said as she tapped the blank screen. "How do you turn this damn thing on?" When the phone ignored her commands, she tossed it at me. The black screen glowed blue the moment I caught it. "How did you do that?" she asked.

"Do what?"

"Phone ignored me completely. Is it locked or something?"

I shook my head and placed the phone in her waiting hands. When Alyce pulled up the text messages, she paled. "You were working on your paper with-with Greg? Basement dorm-dweller of creepitude?"

"He's really not that bad. He knows a lot about economics."

"And serial killers. Are you nuts? Wait, don't answer that." She frowned as Q-Be waved a white flag at her. "Least you had the common sense not to meet in his dorm room."

I didn't bother to mention we were meeting there tomorrow after class. Besides, it wasn't anything weird—most of his books were in his dorm room, and I still had midterms to get through.

No need to worry her all over again.

WHEN PROFESSOR SNAP-PANTS handed me my paper facedown, I assumed the worst and took the crash position—head crouched close to my chest and eyes squinting as I raised one corner of the paper ever so slowly. A few red squiggles corrected a typo or three, and I winced.

"Relax, Ms. Jenkins," Professor Snap-Pants said with a smile. "Yours was one of the better papers this time."

I flipped over the page in a rush. A-minus. An actual A-freaking-minus. The dance I did in my seat resembled Q-Be's a bit too much. Not that anyone else would know that. My cheeks warmed anyway.

The remaining lecture flew through one ear and out the other as my thoughts drifted back to last night. While Alyce sat through her one evening class this semester, I'd watched Greg's favorite movie on his 40-inch flat screen. I'd heard the lines enough times to feel like I'd seen it, but there's nothing like a little blood spray across the screen to push you into reality. It hadn't been as creepy as I'd thought, but hearing Greg quote the lines under his breath had left me with goose bumps.

Still, Alyce and I could recite every line to certain musicals, so maybe Greg wasn't all *that* bad, I guess.

I was three feet out the classroom door when my phone buzzed.

How'd you do on your paper? texted Greg.

Tell ya shortly.

When I turned the corner, I collided into a blue collared shirt that smelled of sweat and earl gray tea. "Alyce! Look!" I shouted as I shoved the paper in her face. "I got an A-minus on my paper!"

"The one Basement Giant helped you with?" She'd taken to calling him that again. "Good. Maybe now you'll ditch the third wheel."

She brushed me aside as she ducked into a nearby classroom. Was that a fight? Had we ever had a real fight? Q-Be buzzed in my pocket, but I ignored it. Tears stung my eyes, and I blinked them away. A glance at my wristwatch warned me I would be late if I didn't hustle.

I'd have to explain it all to Alyce later.

"SHE DOESN'T UNDERSTAND YOU," I said as I sprawled, legs tossed across the recliner's arm.

Greg focused on the animated fox on the flat screen. "Maybe she's jealous," he said as he jabbed at the game controller's buttons. "I mean, I am a worthy opponent."

"Alyce doesn't get jealous." He laughed, and I said, "No, really."

The fox flew a spaceship across the screen, and Greg gave a triumphant shout as the credits rolled. I glanced at my phone and brushed a thumb across it to summon Q-Be.

HOW CAN I ASSIST YOU?

I was tempted to say, fix my love life, but not in front of Greg. Besides, there was no reason for jealousy. Greg was just a friend.

Q-Be sent a little heart across the screen. What I needed was a good cat video. It'd been ages since I'd watched one, and they were certainly better than Greg's games. I tapped the CatTube app, and a pop-up appeared.

WATCH VIDEOS IN 3-D ON YOUR PHONE. 99¢ TODAY ONLY.

I swiped the ad away and another replaced it.

SHOW HIM YOU CARE WITH 3-D VIDEOS.

Dammit. I was NOT in love with Greg.
I wasn't.

ARE YOU SURE?

Q-Be's pointed eyebrows appeared at the edge of the phone's screen. "Go away!" I shouted.

The controller dangled from Greg's hands. "Are you all right?"

"Oh shit, I didn't mean—I wasn't talking to you."

"Then who?"

Good question. I held up my phone in his direction. "Q-Be."

"Oh, you have that app, too?" On the television screen, the fox gave a thumbs-up before the screen faded to black. "You know, I can't find any reference to him in the app store. Weird, huh?"

"Then how'd you get it?"

"It was already installed on my phone when I got it," said Greg as he set the controller on the end table. "What about you?"

The bottom of my stomach dropped a good foot. "I figured you'd installed it."

"Me? Why me?"

"Well, because... you know, you got me the phone."

Greg shook his head. "It wasn't from me. It's part of the study."

Vomit rose in the back of my throat, and Greg's video game haven swam in a pool of blurry cartridges and blue-glowing electronics. "Greg, you had to have sent me the phone. Alyce said it was from you."

"Nope. She passed me in the mail room, and I..."

"You had my mail waiting for me."

His cheeks flushed almost maroon against the rest of his pale skin. "Yeah."

"Wait—you mentioned a study. What study? Where'd you get your phone?" Q-Be vibrated a large exclamation point, which I dismissed. Another alert popped up, and I shoved the phone in my pocket.

"I got my phone from the same place you did. Look—all of this was disclosed in the study agreement. Did you read it at all?"

After ignoring my pulsing phone, an auditory alert shrieked a fire alarm sound, and I yanked the phone from my pocket. "What?!"

A message from Greg wavered at the screen's top. *Hey, wanna work on some more economics? Midterms are coming up.*

"No, Greg," I said aloud. "We're having a conversation. Besides, don't you think we studied enough yesterday?"

He asked, "What are you talking about?"

"Your text."

"My what?"

"Your text message. About studying?"

Greg's nose bunched up as he stared at me. "Mikala, I didn't send you a text message."

"Then what's this?" I asked as I thrust the phone into his face. He squinted as he read the message, then paled.

"I don't know what kind of joke you're playing, Mikala, but I didn't send that. My phone's still in my bag."

I glanced in the corner where his worn out satchel took up most of the desk's real estate. The corner of his phone poked out from beneath the flap. My phone vibrated, and I glanced down to see another message.

I can help you study.

It wasn't Greg. My stomach clawed its way up my esophagus and left a trail of bile that burned my tonsils. *Who is this?* I texted back.

Let me help you, Mikala. 99¢ today only! Q-Be waved at me. Then he disappeared.

"Where'd he go?" I asked.

"Who?"

"Q-Be."

Greg leaned over my shoulder to better look at my phone. "Did you pay the money to get him back?"

"Okay, what the hell, Greg. It's bad enough to be getting random messages from-not-you, but I gotta pay to get that bouncing cube back?"

"Well, you don't *have* to, but yeah. The makers must have put an expiration date on his free time."

I passed my phone to Greg, text message screen visible, and asked, "Doesn't that look like you?"

His finger scrolled through the texts, fast at first and then slowing as his frown deepened. "Half of these are mine, but... but some of these aren't me. I mean, some of them are... well..."

"Creepy?"

"Yeah."

He crossed to his desk and slung one strap of his satchel over his shoulder. "I've got somewhere to be. Feel free to let yourself out." Greg was out the door before my mouth fell open.

What the hell? First I'd managed to piss off Alyce and now Greg?

And I had no idea how I'd done either. And what the hell study was Greg talking about?

My eyes fell on my phone.

BRING BACK Q-BE? JUST 99¢. Y/N

My thumb hovered over the Y a moment before it fell on the screen.

BACK IN MY DORM ROOM—MY empty-of-Alyce dorm room—I had two choices. I could study for my economics quiz, or I could figure out where Alyce was and pull my life back together. As much as I wanted to do the latter, Q-Be's persistence by way of pop-ups reminded me of my grade. Not even the A-minus on my paper had pulled me out of the C zone, so I sprawled across my bed with every intention of studying.

I glanced at my phone where Q-Be waved, flipped, then waved again. "What?" I said, and he stopped, little stick hands on his hips.

WOULD YOU LIKE HELP STUDYING? Y/N

Why the hell not. I jabbed the Y.

FOR 99¢, I CAN FIND YOU A TUTOR. WOULD YOU LIKE TO TRY IT?

No. I had one tutor too many in my life at the moment, gee, thanks.

FOR 99¢, Q-BE CAN TURN ON TUTOR MODE. WOULD YOU LIKE TO TRY IT?

Q-Be tutors? It wasn't like 99 cents was a deal-breaking amount, but if the little guy was gonna charge me for every action, I'd run through my spare cash faster than Alyce and Tom's Chips. But if I didn't pay up, I'd be stuck studying alone.

I paid the money. Q-Be rotated and swelled until he transformed into a large textbook, which opened to display a busy day at the stock exchange.

---

*A **stock exchange** is a stock market where brokers and traders can buy and/or sell stocks (also called shares), bonds, and other securities. Stock exchanges may provide facilities for redemption of securities and other financial and capital events such as payment of income and dividends.*

I sighed. Even Q-Be regurgitated dry text like Professor Snap-Pants, and I'd paid 99 cents for the privilege. "Q-Be, could you make this a little more... I don't know, fun?"

FOR 99¢, Q-BE CAN ACTIVATE THE LEARNING ZONE. WOULD YOU LIKE TO TRY IT?

My thumb tapped the Y, and the stock exchange's rear doors swung open. Q-Be flew inside, taking the camera with him, and landed in a neon-painted exchange. Cartoon traders bounced, shouting about their day trades in tiny, squeaking voices. Q-Be gestured for me to touch the balloon, and when I did, the market cheered. "You've unlocked a math game!"

Oh goodie. I thought the learning zone would be for... you know, learning. Next thing you know, the damn app would broadcast reality shows. I tossed my phone aside and glanced at the clock. If I left now, I'd be early for class, but it was better than math games and balloons.

I grabbed my jacket on my way out the door. Quiz time, ready or not.

THE GOOD THING ABOUT PROFESSOR SNAP-PANTS' quizzes: you knew what your grade was before you left class. Dude was keen on peer grading. *(More time at the beach for him?)* The bad thing about

Professor Snap-Pants' quizzes—you knew what your grade was before you left class.

When the pizza-breath student across from me handed back my paper, it wasn't a C. It was a whopping twenty-five, in fact. An F. The professor called for everyone to pass their pages forward, and for a moment, I considered crumbling mine into a ball instead. But a twenty-five was better than a zero, so I slid my notebook paper—ratty edges and all—into the stack heading toward the Professor's waiting hands.

My tears blurred the hallway outside into a mess of colors and sunlight. Q-Be had failed me. Even worse, I had failed me. When someone bumped into my shoulder, I muttered a quick sorry as I stumbled out of the way.

"Wait, Mikala, hold up!" Alyce caught my hand at the T-junction. "What's wrong?"

I held up my phone where another pop-up message reminded me that I could study for the midterm by paying to unlock another room in Q-Be's library. "Damn thing keeps taking my money, and now I've failed my economics quiz, which probably means I'll fail the midterm and then the class, and I can't afford to do that because then they'll take away my scholarships and kick me out of college, and my granny would kill me and kick me out too, and then what will I do?" I sucked in air too fast and choked on my own saliva.

Typical—just like the rest of my life—a clusterfusk. I shoved my phone into my jacket pocket.

Alyce wrapped her arms around me and pulled me close. The smell of earl gray tea soothed my frantic breaths. Somewhere in my pocket, my phone vibrated. Q-Be could go to hell. The phone persisted, and Alyce slid her hand into the offending pocket. "Why's Greg texting you?" she whispered into my ear.

"It's not Greg. It's probably Q-Be."

She stepped away from me, my phone in her hand. "App's named Greg?"

"No, it's pretending to be Greg."

One moment we were standing in the hall and the next, Alyce had pulled me outside and across campus to our dormitory. Her nose twitched as she marched me down the stairs. "Where are we going?" I asked.

"Greg's. I've had it with this creep, and this app of his."

I should've corrected her about the app, but I figured it would all come out in a moment anyway. In the background, Kevin Spacey gave his monologue to Brad Pitt as Greg's favorite movie blared. When he didn't respond to Alyce's knocks, she kicked at the wooden door. Third kick, the door opened to display a bleary-eyed Greg. Either he'd been crying, or he'd been cutting some fierce onions.

"Remove your app from the phone you sent her," Alyce snapped. Greg trudged to his futon and dropped into it with all the effort of a slug. "Did you hear me, Basement Giant?"

He muttered something under his breath.

Alyce grabbed the remote from the table. "Answer me, or Kevin goes bye-bye."

"Not my app. Not my phone. NOT MY PROBLEM."

I'd never heard him shout before. "Alyce, it's not his app. It's on his phone, too."

"Well, yeah, 'cause he made it. Look, Mikala, the app isn't available in the app store. It doesn't exist outside Greg."

"Sure it does," I said, but Alyce was already shaking her head.

"Damn thing doesn't exist. Google it. It's not there—no reference to it anywhere, and that's not normal."

Huh. Everything was online these days. Maybe this study contained a secret app? I shook my head. Highly unlikely—there are laws about things like that. "That still doesn't mean he made it. Greg mentioned a study earlier. He got a new phone because of it, right?"

"Yeah, but I tossed it." Greg flipped off the flat screen by feel. "Damn thing kept spamming me with banner ads and pop-ups for that damn cube thing. I don't need the money *that* bad."

"Why didn't you uninstall the app?" asked Alyce, and he rolled his red-rimmed eyes. "What?"

"That was the first thing I tried. Uninstalled and five minutes later, the banner ads multiplied. They spread into every app on my phone. I couldn't even log in to input the grades for Professor Frederick, which, by the way, Mikala, what happened?"

"Ad-splosion."

Greg picked at a nub on his maroon and blue striped sweater. Alyce claimed a seat beside him on his couch. "Greg?" Perspiration broke out across his forehead as he met her gaze. From where I stood, her legs brushed against his jeans as she turned on her best smile. Resistance was futile. "Are you sure you didn't make this app?"

His skin tried to meld with the pea-green cushion. "I swear, it wasn't me."

Alyce fiddled with my phone, then swore.

"I told you, the banners just spread. It's like a virus," he said.

"Hey, my phone's gotta virus scanner on it." I held out my hand for my phone, but Alyce pushed my hand aside.

"Downloaded the scanner from Q-Be, didn't you?" she asked, and I nodded. Seemed like everything on my new phone was Q-Be connected in some way.

It was the quietest I'd ever heard Greg's dorm. For someone without any friends, he lived a loud life with his movies and games. Alyce scooched away from him and set my phone on the end table. "So tell me about this study."

Greg shrugged. "It's a campus study on technology usage. Participants get a free phone that records their actions, spending habits, and stress levels. All the details were in the contract—"

My brain tickled, and I held up a finger. "Greg, I never signed any contract. Hell, I'd never heard of the study until you mentioned it today."

"That's impossible. Professor Frederick said you needed some extra credit—"

"Wait, that's where the phone came from?" I asked.

He nodded. "I assume so. You got the box with the phone, so it must be."

Alyce stood and pulled me towards the door. "Greg, where would this professor be right now?"

"His office or maybe one of the dorm mail rooms." At our puzzled looks, he added, "You know, dropping off more phones for the study."

"Sounds like it's field trip time," Alyce said and pulled me into the hallway. Greg was half a second behind us.

IF THERE WAS one place Alyce hated more than Greg's dorm, it was his supposed domain—the mailroom. When he wasn't blaring serial killer movies, he stalked the mailroom in hopes of tempting some co-ed or another into having an actual conversation with him. These past few weeks, he'd come off as less a creep and more a pathetic grad student.

As we strode into the mailroom, its three occupants fled with down gazes and shrinking postures. To some, he'd always be the creepy Basement Giant.

I pulled a brown box out of the cubby. "This looks just like the box my phone arrived in, sans the rain."

When Alyce pointed at the familiar blue stamp, she said, "The study's university-approved. How'd he get permission to mess with students' minds and money? I mean, you didn't sign any contracts or waivers, so what gives?"

"We can't go blaming him without proof that he's done something wrong." I shoved the package back into the student's mailbox. "Can we?"

"We've got all the proof we need." Alyce held up my phone. "How much have you spent on this app?"

Greg shook his head and said, "You can't go after him for the freemium model. Most apps work that way these days. It's not Professor Frederick's fault Mikala chose to spend the money. Or... maybe it is." Greg spun around and fled the mailroom. Alyce and I followed behind, reaching his dorm room out of breath and confused.

"What?" I asked.

He waved his hand in my general direction as he booted up his laptop and navigated his browser to the university staff website. "Turn around," he said.

"Why?" I asked.

"Password privacy."

Alyce and I rolled our eyes at each other and turned away from his screen. For a moment, only the clacking of computer keys sounded until Greg let out a loud, "Ah-ha!"

I bumped into Alyce's elbow as we both turned. Greg had logged into the staff portal and pulled up the approval letter for the study. "How'd you get that?" I asked.

"It's part of the university's new transparency goal. All staff can review currently approved studies by other staff. Keeps them honest or something. Or maybe it was about idea theft. Eh." He waved his hand at no one in particular. "Either way, the study description—read it."

"'Description of Study (please include the means by which data will be gathered): This study will be used to evaluate cell-phone micro-transactions and their impact on the economy, specifically the micro-economy established within the university. Participants in the study will receive a phone pre-loaded with applications useful for college students. While students will be prompted to unlock various portions of the app via purchases, no money will be collected. The application will appear to accept the information while all personal data will be deleted.'" I shrugged when I finished reading.

"We've got him. He's stealing money. Isn't that fraud?" asked Alyce.

As Greg nodded, I said, "Nope. None of the transactions have touched my bank account... at least not yet. But we do have him—just not the reason you two think." I pointed to the project's parameter checklist. "Look, one of the requirements of all research studies is that they can't be tied with student grades in any way. Professor Snap-Pants told Greg I needed extra credit, and suddenly I had a phone. I didn't sign any waivers, either."

Alyce took a screen shot of the approval form. "Now all we have to do is report him to the people for the ethical treatment of studies or something," she said.

The tension in my stomach returned. I wasn't sure reporting him for an ethics violation was the best way to handle it. After all, he'd been trying to do what I asked—give me extra credit. Alyce nudged me with her elbow. "You've got anxiety face," she said.

"I—I'm not sure about jumping straight to the reporting stage. Maybe he doesn't know how crazy the study has gotten, or maybe he doesn't remember the bit about the grades. Look, my granny is always saying that adults work it out. Or they try to, anyway. Maybe we should talk to him first."

Both wore expressions that were a mix of disbelief and outright exasperation, but they followed me just the same. The glaring sunlight outside the dorm reminded me of Q-Be's bouncy, happy self. Maybe this was all just a misunderstanding.

I had a sinking feeling in my gut... sinking like my grades. Maybe he'd be willing to give me that extra credit before turning himself in to the provost. Somehow I doubted it.

GREG LED us to Rogers Hall: home of economics majors everywhere and Professor Snap-Pants' office. Being a freshman class, Economics 101 was held in an auditorium in the business building, so I'd had no purpose in visiting it often. I'd only been there the once, a week before all the Q-Be craze, and then only to drop off a candy bar for a sleep-deprived friend. At the time, the hallways had been filled with one too many button-up shirts and ties for me.

Rather than the business school norm, a throng of students in *bad* need of a shower gathered at the front entrance. In their hands—shiny new Micro-Lunia IIIs. "Where did you get those?" I asked as I elbowed my way through the crowd.

"Professor Frederick handed them out in class."

"But why are y'all standing out here?" Alyce asked from over my shoulder.

"Q-Be's giving out a prize to folks standing in these exact coordinates... or maybe it's two feet this way... we're not sure." The student glanced down at his feet and took a small step to the left. Then he swiped a finger across his phone and shrugged. The group followed his movements en masse.

A triad of major chords filled the air, and student cheered. "Achievement unlocked! Look, Q-Be's got cheevos!" He held his phone in the air which displayed a silver trophy and the catch phrase, "Q-Be, it's where U-be!"

With the students moving away, Greg motioned us through the doors before the greasy-haired, baggy-eyed Q-Be addicts remembered our existence. I caught the quick glances Alyce shot my way and groaned. "Was I that bad?"

She sniffed the shoulder of my shirt where a bit of dried *something* remained, then shrugged as if to say *you tell me*. Greg led us up the stairs and down a mostly empty corridor. Muffled voices reached us from inside classrooms as we passed. The doorway to the professor's office stood cracked open at the hall's end.

"Now what?" Alyce whispered.

"Come in. I can't stand students who stand outside and whisper as if I'm deaf." Professor Snap-Pants' rumbling voice made me flinch, but my false bravado forced me to push open his office door.

Rather than the piles of papers strewn across the desk and wall-lined books I'd expected, his office was eerily neat and spartan. Not a single dust particle out of place. I wanted to ask him if he'd ever used the office before today, but Alyce cleared her throat.

"Um, Professor, I... uh, I'm sorry to bother you, but I wanted to ask you about the study," I said.

"Yes? It should help your grade some, Ms. Jenkins, though I would suggest you work harder if you plan to pass with more than a C." He glanced up at Greg and said, "My TA here is an excellent tutor. Perhaps you could ask him for some assistance."

"Sir, I already did that, but that's not really why I'm here."

Alyce snapped out her phone and shoved it towards the professor, who pulled reading glasses out of his wind jacket pocket. He stared at the phone a moment, then shrugged. "I see you've convinced my TA to pull up study details." He turned back to a book on his desk.

"I'm sorry, sir," Greg said as he tapped the man on the shoulder, "but we were looking at the form and, well, you seem to have broken the university's rules with your study."

It wasn't a professor who spun around in his chair, but a fierce-eyed man whose bushy brows twitched and lips turned down at their corners. Despite the change, his voice remained level. "And what do you suppose you'll do with this information? You think the provost is unaware of this study? Or how it operates? That piece of paper is a mere formality to appease the university donors. Nothing more."

"Sir, I was hoping you'd do the right thing—"

He laughed at me.

And I stood there and took it. He held my grade in my hands and in that moment, I was small.

He saw it and pounced. He rose from his chair, the snap-buttons of his pants straining against his muscles. "Who are you, Ms. Jenkins, to demand anything of me? Freshmen do not make the rules at this university." He turned then to Greg. "And neither do former TAs. Now get out of my office before I call campus security."

The way the professor glared at me sent my feet tumbling backward until I hit the doorframe. I wasn't about to tangle with security, so I righted myself and fled his office. The rattle and boom of a slamming door reached me at the hallway's end, and shortly after, so did Greg and Alyce.

"Why didn't you say something? You don't have to take that shit from him!" said Alyce.

"You don't get it. If he'd called security, who you think they're gonna believe? Black freshman me, or some wealthy white tenured professor? We should've kept our mouths shut." Greg's hands clenched into fists, and I said, "I'm sorry you lost your TA position."

Alyce draped her arm about my shoulder. Greg pushed open the double doors and once outside, took off at a run. "Where's he going?" asked Alyce.

"No idea."

Ten feet away, a smelly student bounced his phone off the sidewalk as we passed. "Cheap piece of shit," he muttered. The crowd had dwindled to half, and phones littered the entryway.

"What happened?" asked Alyce.

"Q-Be up and died or something," said one student whose thumbs flew over his phone's screen. "I better not have lost all my achievements. I paid good money for those!"

My phone powered up just fine, but no dancing cube wiggled across my screen. No banner ads either. Nothing but the plain old home screen with a few basic apps.

And my ever-dropping grades.

IF IT'D BEEN my choice, I wouldn't have bothered going to class the next day, but Alyce dragged me first out of bed and then out of the dorm. "Look, he's an asshole. He's a white man with all the power; I get it."

She didn't, but I appreciated her trying.

"Either way, your grade won't get better by itself. Since when have you ever let someone tell you how to be?" she asked as she pulled me towards the auditorium. "You fought like hell for your scholarship. Get in there and fight like it for your grade. Let him know he's beneath you. Didn't your granny teach you what to do 'bout bullies?"

Despite my sour mood, I smiled.

"Go on, say it." Alyce nudged me with her elbow. "Do it."

Gran might as well have kicked me in the tail—her honey breath whispered the words across my shoulder. "Nobody be happy 'til they shoved you 'neath that dirt. Is why you gotta be brave and stannup. Don't be givin' your power 'way to none."

I spoke the words aloud before the closed classroom door. I'd never gotten anything less than an A, never given less than my best, and I'd certainly never given up my power. But then, I'd never had so much to lose. As I opened the door, Alyce stood behind me *(though I suspect she was there to make sure I didn't make a speedy exit)*.

No one looked up as I entered. They were all too busy on their phones.

I took a seat toward the rear as Greg entered with the university's provost. When he spotted me, he shot me a quick thumbs-up before clearing his throat. The provost wore a button-up blazer in navy blue that screamed importance, though her gaze fidgeted back and forth between the class and Greg. When she spoke, a sea of heads tilted up as one.

"Professor Frederick will be unable to continue the semester as planned. His TA will take over for the remainder until a replacement can be found. You will, of course, be given a brief survey about Mr. Klevine's performance at the semester's end."

Greg tried to bury his neck in his shoulders as she shot him a concerned look. Once she left the room, a dozen questions rang out.

"Will his leaving impact our grades? He promised to get me into this study for extra credit. Sounded fun..."

"Is Q-Be gone as well? I had cheevos, you see..."

"Will we get a refund for the money spent on the study? Tuition payments are due..."

The questions focused on the stupid app, and I raised my hand. When Greg called on me, I asked, "What happened to the professor? Is he all right?"

"He's gone. Office all packed up, and his home's empty. No one has a clue what happened. Poor bastard." Greg winced. "Sorry about the vocabulary. I'd just hate to think something might've happened to him, is all."

Goosebumps marched across my bare arms. Had Greg done something to Professor Snap-Pants? When I caught Greg's gaze, he smiled the typical lopsided Greg grin. The smile said, "Trust me, I'm harmless."

There was something my granny always said about "quiet folks"—something about their shouts being the loudest. Before I could think on it further, my phone vibrated in my jean pocket. All around me, phones chirped, beeped, buzzed, and trilled.

1 new email.

I swiped my finger across the screen, and the short message pulled up.

Message from: Professor Frederick
Subject: Final grades
As we approach midterms, you should be thinking about your final grades. Your current grade is: 90. There is no extra credit in this class, but if you'd like to discuss ways to improve your grade, my office hours are MW 10 a.m.-12 p.m.

Professor Frederick

Whispers spread as students read their emails. The time stamp was from ten minutes ago. Unless he'd changed his mind about my average and set up some auto-email thingy before disappearing, the email made no sense. I pulled away from my phone long enough to see Greg grin before facing the dry erase board. A girl beside me tapped me on the arm, and I yelped.

"Sorry. Did your grade change?" she asked.

"Yeah. Weird, huh?"

"I guess. Oh well, gift horses' mouths and all that. You know?" She returned to her phone, and I caught some mumble or another about sharing the news on social media.

All around me, heads bowed to their phones while Greg scribbled notes on the board with a blue, dry-erase marker. My phone vibrated again with another text message, sender unknown. *Smile, Mikala. It's the grade you deserve.*

Had the email been from Professor Snap-Pants at all? And what about the anonymous text?

Greg cleared his throat. "If you'll turn in your books to page 192."

Maybe Alyce had been right about Basement Giant.

Maybe she'd been right about a lot of things.

"Oh, hey, while I'm thinking about it"—Greg paused, marker raised —"if you're struggling and need a little help, I found this great app last night..."

ABOUT "Q-BE"

Originally published in *Untethered: A Magic iPhone Anthology* (Cantina Publishing), "Q-Be" came from one too many conversations with my partner about the *Freemium* Model in App development. Nothing is free. *Nothing.* Everything has a price, so for this anthology about tech gone wrong, I explored the idea of why freemium is evil. Outside of tie-in fiction, it was also my first short story to be traditionally published.

HANDS

EVEN WHEN I'M SLEEPING, I feel them. Each whorled digit pressed ever so slightly against my throat, ten fingers that pierce like porcupine quills at the base of my skull. I count sheep to pretend I'm alone.

When the buzzing in my brain finally quiets around the 3 AM mark and I drift into the unsteady rhythm my body calls sleep, the hands are an ever present reminder of every failure and every task left in a rumpled pile at the foot of my bed.

At 7 AM, the alarm in my brain morphs from a soft signal to a blaring battle horn and by 7:10, I am upright and as bleary as the sun on the horizon. The white tile floor is cold beneath my bare feet. Though I stand outside the protection of the bedsheets and goosebumps tickle the parts of me still flesh, I pause outside the bedroom door.

Nothing moves, not yet.

I glance back at the safety of my bed. It sits in the corner, warm and waiting, but if I return to it, an ocean of tears will keep me company. It would wake him.

His chest rises and falls in a steadiness I will never know. But then, he doesn't carry the weight of these hands slung 'round my neck. To share my worries would be to hang him with the same noose—a punishment befitting no one. Yet to remain silent is to carry this weight alone.

My brain tires of my melancholy and sends the signal. My silver-laden hand responds against my will. The door opens and my metallic leg steps forward, dragging my skin along for the ride. I open my mouth to yell, but my brain refuses to leave the peace and quiet behind and so no sound beyond the exhalation of air is made. There's a rhythm to the thunk-drag, thunk-draaaaag I make as I shuffle down the hall to the bathroom. This door opens automatically, and for now, I'm propelled by my bladder's urge to rid itself of waste.

A mix of water and urine swirl down the bowl, and the fingers around my neck squeeze. A gentle reminder to breathe.

Could I go? Down the pipes and out into a world of harsh colors and harsher people?

I turn away from the toilet and catch myself in a mirror of cracks spiderwebbing out from the point of impact. My head still resembles peach fuzz, but the pallor of my skin lights a stark contrast to the metal. Once my arm and leg had been shiny—brand new chrome with blinking lights and marble joints.

Once, it had been cool to walk again. To hug someone, even if touching them—a rough interpretation of zeroes and ones—felt like running my face into a concrete wall.

I was the one. The one who survived.

My body resumes its shamble past a long row of doors that ignore me as I pass. My shoulders slump. I can feel them again—there. The grip tightens.

The simplest action is impossible, yet my heart ramps up its maniacal drumbeat the closer I am to the hallway's end.

Rough and ragged, my open mouth rips the air from around me as I pass through the archway. Here is where we argue, with pans tossed into a dirty sink and the refrigerator door hanging open at an odd angle. "I'm worried," I said last night, and he blinked as if the world suddenly stopped and began rotating counter-clockwise. Worry is a daily occurrence.

Worry is an inconvenience.

Bile rises in my throat at the memory, and it burns on the way back down.

I hold my hands out in front of me—one metal, one flesh—and

wrap them around my throat, my thumbs digging into my lymph nodes. When I let go, the pressure remains. I am not alone.

My brain kicks into overdrive to push me towards the refrigerator where I stare at a random ensemble of milk, two-week-old leftovers, and a moldy orange. I could have sworn there was food... Or was that last week? When did we last order groceries?

Sweat runs down the side of my face, while the chill of the refrigerator sends goosebumps up my arm.

"There's no food."

His voice startles me, and I fall back against the counter as the hands tighten. When his fingers press against my collarbone, I concentrate on breathing. In. Out. Not as fast as my racing heart, but slow enough to stop my feet from fleeing to the bedroom, to the safety of the bed covers.

"I didn't mean to startle you," he says as he kisses my forehead. "Feel any better today?"

"Define better." The crumbling words fall from my dry, cracked lips, and I grab a cup from the counter to fill with water. I can eat water for breakfast. Better than the nothing I had the day before.

His fingers leave an invisible path down my metal arm as he checks the graph at my wrist. "Calm down. When did you eat last?"

"Yesterday? The day before?" I shrug.

He kicks the refrigerator shut with his heel and opens the pantry. A muffled curse reaches me, then he returns with a cereal box bearing an overly enthusiastic clown on the front. He pours some into a bowl and hands it to me.

"Dry?" I ask, and he nods.

"You're probably not up to rancid milk yet."

I can't help it. The corners of my mouth lift in a momentary smile.

"Once I graduate, you figure I'll be ready for stale pancakes with moldy oranges?" I ask.

He laughs, and for the first time in a long time, the hands around my neck loosen their grip.

I am not alone.

I am not alone.

I whisper the mantra as a metal finger shoves a honey-nut 'O' into my mouth. The fingers hear me as they fade into the background.

"I am not alone."

ABOUT "HANDS"

A few years ago I saw an art exhibit where the artist had interpreted mental illness into art. As someone who suffers from anxiety and panic attacks, it was fascinating to see their interpretation of what anxiety looks like. This made my writer brain contemplate what anxiety would smell like. Taste like. *Feel* like. The story "Hands" is what came from those thoughts.

OL' ST. NICK

Jolly Old Saint Nicholas,
Lean your ear this way;
Don't you tell a single soul
What I'm going to say,
Christmas Eve is coming soon;
Now my dear old man,
Whisper what you'll bring to me;
Tell me if you can.
When the clock is striking twelve,
When I'm fast asleep,
Down the chimney broad and black
With your pack you'll creep;
All the stockings you will find
Hanging in a row;
Mine will be the shortest one;
You'll be sure to know.

—Original lyrics as published in 1881

THE HOLE-RIDDLED SHIP reminded me of my Gran--broken and just a touch too old to remain in an ever-changing world. I'd seen many a battered ship, but standing on the bridge with nothing but a spacesuit between me and possible--scratch that, *probable*--death, set my stomach turning.

Two walls of the bridge were intact, though their computer displays--the undamaged ones, anyway--lay unresponsive. I floated near a hole as tall as me where something had ripped its way through the transport ship's shields and into the hull.

Treaty negotiations between Earth and the New Jhovens left union crews unwilling to contract with freelancers like me. That left my crew and I with salvage work like this. The creepiest kind of work.

Unsettling or not, this job was perfect. Honest theft as these folks had no need of their ship anymore. Besides, we needed the gig. If I had to stomach another protein bar for dinner, I'd be tempted to abandon my *own* damned ship.

Maybe it was *too* perfect. A ship that size, you'd expect someone to miss her or at least miss her crew. If nothing else, word of the attack should have reached someone.

Yet the *Lucky Fish* stood empty--except for my meager crew who floated about scavenging for anything worth selling or using to repair my ship, *The Perffaith*.

Jake's shadow darkened the computer display in front of me. "Fight like this, makes me wonder if there's injured on board."

Half-fix-this, half-carry-that, Jake was my go-to man, though currently he was my *dig-for-parts* man as we combed the *Lucky Fish's* bridge.

"Body scans came up negative for life forms. If anyone's injured, they're long past needing our help, Jake."

"As we boarded, Lissa thought there might be unfriendlies on board. Maybe left over from the fight."

When I turned, his spacesuit's helmet light nailed me directly in the face. I winced, and he tapped a button at his wrist to dim it. "Sorry, Captain," he said.

"If you're that concerned, run another scan."

Jake shook his handheld. "Can't. Scanner's dead again."

No heat sources registered, not even ours, and I swore.

"There are all manner of species that don't read right on our scanners--*provided they work*--so no sense in being lax with security, sir."

I winced at his paraphrasing. "Remind me to give you the job if I ever need a new security officer. You nailed Lissa's deadpan perfectly." Her uptight personality used to be a boon. Now it was just a reminder of our past.

My suit's thick, synthetic fibers protected my fingers from the jagged metal hole in front of me. Jake pulled himself closer until he reached my side, his blond dreads mashed up against his sweaty face. "This is one battle I'm sure glad we missed."

Despite the fresh shave, my black scalp itched as sweat trickled down to my jaw. I glanced at Jake's dreads again.

"Itchy?" he asked.

"Yeah. Must be time to switch out the filters." Yet another thing to add to my growing list of repairs to make whenever we had money again.

"Maybe the *Lucky Fish* will have the parts." Jake's breathing was loud in my helmet's speakers. "I'm glad they ain't here. The stiffs, I mean. Hate when we hafta work around dead folks."

"Open channel two to *The Perffaith*," I spoke into my helmet, which buzzed in response. The channel light flipped to green, connecting me to my chief engineer. "Zac, any luck talking to the computer over here? Or getting her to power up?"

My helmet crackled, and when Zac answered, his voice was louder and clearer than before. "Nope. Something must've blown out the system. I'll need to hop on over to see what's the--"

"Negative, Zac. Remain on board *The Perffaith*." A press of my thumb and index finger closed the channel, and I flipped a power switch on a nearby console. No response. "Gut what you can, Jake. The bridge is a loss. But keep a lookout for the black box."

He removed the protective glass from a panel and set to stripping the innards of anything that didn't show obvious char-marks.

If I could find the black box, maybe I could sort out her last moments... The panel's door below me was fused together. I pushed away from it to float across to a more intact portion of the bridge. One console bore a few scorch marks but little else. The cover almost fell off in my hands, but its insides were a jumble of wires. No box.

"Open channel four." When the light lit, I asked, "Hey, Seb, how's it looking in the cargo hold?"

There was a delay in either the comm or his response. Maybe the *Lucky Fish* was bouncing the signal around. Or maybe our suits sucked. I resisted the urge to rip off my helmet as static squealed in my ears and set them ringing.

"...Salvaged one crate...moved onto--"

"Did you catch any of that, Jake?"

Shoulder deep in computer hardware, he mumbled, "Said something 'bout salvaging a crate."

How helpful.

"Captain, we have an issue." Seb's voice rang too sharp in my ears.

"Report!"

"There is someone unexpected on the ship. A survivor perhaps."

The scanners had gone belly up again. Sweat rolled down my back, and the suit adjusted its humidity levels to compensate. "Where?"

"Unknown, Captain. The heat signature is sporadic."

"Zac--" There was no response on channel two. "Locate Officer Zac Curtis."

A squeal let loose in my helmet and channel five pulsed before autoconnecting. "Captain?"

"Why are you on a suit channel? Hurry up and shut the cargo doors on *The Perffaith*, Zac. I don't need anyone getting any ideas like making off with our ship."

"No-can-do, Captain. I just boarded the *Lucky Fish* to help track our mystery person."

Shit. No one could've survived on this ship full of holes. That left other scrappers. Folks likely to shoot first and ask questions later. At most, I figured we might run across some space critter or another-- usually did on a salvage trip--but nothing humanoid or weapon- carrying.

But then, derelicts and wounded ships attracted the most unsavory types, didn't they?

No misplaced shadows lurked outside the bridge. I snatched a serrated hunk of metal debris floating in front of me and shielded myself as I pushed my way along the corridor. Zac, my chief engineer, met me and Jake at the junction between Hallway A and Corridor C.

Zac gripped a piece of a wooden crate. He'd come from the left instead of the right, and I frowned.

Besides being an excellent engineer, the goofy guy had been my best friend since childhood. He must have guessed my thoughts as he said, "I rechecked the cargo hold on my way to you."

The corridor to engineering was as empty as those to the bridge had been. Outside the engine room, Lissa stood guard. The spacesuit hid her muscular frame, but she was imposing enough with the chill across her face.

"Jake, is Seb showing up on the scanner?" I asked. Jake slapped the device. "Is now."

"You and Zac intercept him. I don't want him tracking this heat source alone."

Both men pulled themselves down the corridor. I stuck my head inside the engine room. Two crew members were waist deep in engine parts. Too busy to notice anything but chipsets and circuitry.

I drifted back into the hall to Lissa, "Seen anything or anyone?"

"Nothing yet."

"Stay with the crew members here."

"But--"

I held up my hand and she *tsked*, something she did more often than I liked. Before she could voice her opinion, my speakers squawked. "Captain, we've got a problem."

"What is it, Zac?"

Silence made me hurry--as much as one could in a spacesuit.

More popping and sputtering from my speakers. Zac's voice returned, halting my forward propulsion. "We found Seb. Damned heat source vanished."

"Vanished? Equipment malfunction?"

I'd replaced all the handheld scanners' memory chips last month. Cheap New Jhovensian shit.

"Worse. Our heat source is freshly dead."

THE ROOM SEB had discovered was little more than a closet. Crates and sacks of goods crowded it beyond cozy, and the dead body splayed through the center took up more than his fair share of space. His round belly floated over a thick, black belt cinching pants stained with grease and who knew what else. Then there was the garish red jacket. Ugly thing with too much fur for this century.

"He is freshly deceased, Captain. The body-- " Seb's voice cracked, "--still bears warmth."

White whiskers were sprinkled across the dead man's broad chin, and his round cherry cheeks were rounder than I remembered. I forced my hand to relax around the hunk of debris I'd grabbed as a makeshift weapon.

Seb's white skin was near translucent as he hovered in the doorway. He was the only non-human on board, but with a pair of stylin' shades over his eyes and his orange afro wig, you could almost think him human. Right up 'til he opened his mouth and spewed something about the sins of freedom and enterprise in his near-perfect English.

He was the newest member of my crew--the most annoying member of my crew--but right now, I didn't blame him for getting a case of the wiggins.

Petrie, my medical officer, squeezed past him. Her hip brushed his leg, and Seb flinched. "Back away from the body, please," said Petrie. She crouched with a grunt as the crew watched. A sour smell left my tongue too thick in my mouth.

"You good, Cap?" asked Zac.

I blinked several times to clear my head. "Unnecessary complications bug me is all."

"So what happened to him, Doc?"

Petrie glanced at Zac, then returned her attention to the victim. "I'll need to do a full autopsy to be sure, but I suspect he asphyxiated."

"What's the scanner say about that heat source now, Zac? If someone on board killed this man, it's not too far a stretch to think they might kill someone else," I said.

He held up his scanner. The blue grid held a dozen heat sources, every last one of them traceable to the trackers in our suits.

Seb glared at the functioning scanner. "I followed the foreign heat source here before it disappeared. This tells me the man who appeared as an additional heat source is the one lying before us."

"Ya really think someone offed him, Mark? I mean, ship's pretty damaged--what's one more stiff on a ship like this?" Jake asked.

Our dead man lacked a beard the last time I saw him. I blinked away the memory and said, "There's something odd about this whole thing. Between the body, the sensors... This man was alive before we boarded, but how? There's no spacesuit. No air."

"So how'd he breathe? You're right, Cap. Something stinks," said Zac.

"Murder or not, we'll make a full sweep of the *Lucky Fish*." I opened a channel to Lissa. "Get the crew and whatever they salvaged over to *The Perffaith*, then join me in canvassing the *Lucky Fish's* bow. And keep your eyes open."

"Roger that."

"Zac, Seb, search the stern. I'll work from the bridge back."

Both frowned. "I would best seek with you, Captain."

"You're with Zac, Seb."

"But--"

Zac petted Seb on the shoulder. "Don't sweat it. Captain here works best *without* our advice. You'll get used to it."

I flicked Zac on the shoulder, though with my gloves it came out more a tap. I caught his grimace before it disappeared behind his gloved hand.

"I do not understand."

"Give it time. You'll learn to love this ship and its crazy crew once you've been here a while. We rib each other--which means we joke a lot. I know your people aren't so much with the jokes, but you'll adjust," I said. With a nod to Zac, we set out to hunt for a possible survivor...or murderer. Between the debris and bulky spacesuits--I couldn't afford the good stuff--the search was slow going. Other than a few bodies that hadn't been wrenched into space during the fight, no original crewmen remained on the *Lucky Fish*. Our lone heat source was our closeted corpse.

It was a crime worth blowing off, but something nagged me about it. When I returned to the crime scene, a quick search turned up an ID, though I gave it little more than a glance. It was probably fake. Five years and a funny outfit didn't hide those green eyes any more than they hid the scars along his face from one too many brawls.

I dimmed my helmet's visor, blocking out my father's face. It shouldn't have bothered me. We hadn't seen each other in years, and it wasn't like I gave two shits about him. I couldn't afford the distraction. Nevertheless, my jaw ached as I guarded his body. Lissa found me a few minutes later.

"Mark, are you all right?"

"Open channel one--private seal." When the green light inside my helmet flickered, I said to Lissa, "Check out the doorway."

She took a moment to study the frame, stopping near the latch. "The door was pried open."

I pointed at one mark in particular. Paint chips remained embedded in the metal. "Blue paint. *Our* blue paint."

She frowned. "You don't know that for a fact."

"Who else uses Cadmium Blue #20 to label their tools? That's not the normal color used out here. Freelancers Guild uses Cedar Green #8 by and large."

Her gloved fingers flicked a large paint chip from the gouge and sent it drifting into an open bag she held. "It's a common paint color, Captain. For other things at least."

Two channels lit amber in my helmet's display. "Release privacy status," I said and spotted Zac floating toward us with Seb a foot behind.

"Captain, ship's clear as clear can be," said Zac. Seb confirmed the clear status with a nod.

Lissa handed me the key card to the victim's room.

Someone--probably me--was gonna get to dig through his belongings.

"I know I asked before, but are you okay, Mark? You look...shaken," she said.

I turned from that look, a look that wasn't hers to give anymore. Text on the card said Room 5, Level 3. No power meant no lift, so I set out for the emergency stairs. I used the railing to pull myself up until my helmet lamp shined on the number three. When I paused in my ascent, I caught Lissa trailing behind me. "You didn't have to come along."

"You're searching the room."

"Someone has to."

"How do we know it's his room?"

I shrugged. "Not sure, but if nothing else, I'd like to know why he carried the key card."

As we stopped outside room five, I took a deep breath. Like the closet-sized room we'd found him in, the door had been forced open. Pry marks made by something metal had left regular indentations on it. *Unlike* his final resting place, no blue paint chips marred these. I pointed this out to Lissa before we stepped inside.

A fold-up cot filled the majority of the room. Five wall-drawers shared space with a pull-out sink and toilet bowl.

Typical traveler's quarters. I almost laughed to think of someone as flamboyant and crass as Nick living out of a room like this.

I would've figured he'd opt for a suite.

My light reflected off something on the floor, and I rotated upside down to retrieve it. Glass. "Give me a hand," I muttered, and Lissa gave my legs a push 'til I got upright.

"What is it?"

I held it up to our eye level. "Looks like a snow globe. Used to have one of these as a kid." Small, white dust swirled around inside the glass dome and glittered in my light.

She held up an old paperback just as Zac and Seb crossed through the doorway.

"Is that an honest-to-god real book?" asked Zac.

I nodded and set the glass object on the cot. "Real paper, too. I take it your search is done?"

"Yep. Na-da-thing on board but us."

Lissa passed the book to Zac, and he gasped at the cover. "It's our victim!" On the cover, a fat man in a red suit grinned at us. "The Tale of Jolly Ol' Saint Nicholas. Some old artifact from Earth, maybe?"

As much as I hated to admit it, the saint did bear a certain cheesy resemblance to our victim. It was uncanny the way those same green eyes stared back at me, and for a moment, I was a child again and running.

Always running.

"Captain, look." Zac pointed to some text on the front page. "Says here this Saint Nicholas man was some special dignitary on Earth way back when."

There was a cough in my ears. Seb and Jake crowded around the door, hanging on every word Zac uttered as he continued to ramble on about some long dead holiday where folks exchanged gifts and sang about happier times.

"That body isn't a saint. Certainly not some gift-giver," I muttered.

The chatter around me ceased, and Zac cocked his head. "How you figure? Looks like the real deal--the real Santa Claus--to me."

My brain caught up with my mouth. "Too many scars on him. That man's seen too many brawls to be some cheerful saint. I mean, aren't saints supposed to be holy or something?"

Seb asked, "But how would you explain his attire? It is identical to that on the book."

Damn him. The *Alphan* latched onto anything like it was gospel truth. A habit I'd have to break if he wished to remain first mate.

Seb continued, "He even possesses a--what did you call it, Zac? A traditional gift?"

"What gift?"

"The snow globe and book. A find like this might be worth some coin." Zac's eyes glittered in my helmet's light.

"Should we not be worried about how this saint died?" Seb shook the snow globe I'd cast aside earlier, sending white flutters around the tiny city inside.

My stomach threatened to empty itself right there in all that junk. From simple salvage to a crime scene, this job was everything I'd hoped to avoid. Including seeing my father, Nick. Either way, I wasn't gonna be able to walk away without the answer to at least one question: What the hell had Nick been doing on this ship?

"ACCORDING TO HIS IDENTIFICATION, the victim's name is Nick Johnson."

Banes, not Johnson. My brain corrected the details. Why'd he choose Gran's maiden name for his false persona? I ground my teeth as the crew crowded around the body like voyeurs. Petrie, my chief medical officer, rattled more information from her examination as the infirmary display scrolled with data.

Petrie continued, "Until we're able to access the derelict's computer, we won't be able to ascertain his purpose on the *Lucky Fish*. Maybe he's following the old Earth myth of Santa Claus." Eyes the color of weak tea twinkled, lending beauty to an otherwise plain face. "The team found a sack full of Earth artifacts stowed in a crate in the cargo hold."

Knowing Nick, the goods were probably stolen. I swallowed back bile.

"The identification plate on the crate's side matches that of our victim." Petrie pulled back the sheet to expose Nick's face. The swollen, red skin marred the sterile and clinical white room. Like someone had opened a can of animal innards and maraschino cherries, molded them Nick-shaped, and plopped them down on the table.

Lissa's shoulder muscles strained against her blue shirt as she leaned over the victim. She held back her long red braids with one hand and pointed at a pinprick in his neck with the other. "Is this how he died?" she asked.

Petrie pointed again at the large display panel. Scans of various organs scrolled by with a ton of numbers that meant nothing to me. "His toxicology screens show he suffered anoxia--"

At our blank stares, she added, "He asphyxiated as a result of exposure to carbon monoxide."

"When? Seb said we had a heat signature," I interrupted. "The victim was alive when we hailed the *Lucky Fish* and found their computer unresponsive. He died within ten minutes of our coming aboard, so where'd he get the CO exposure?"

"And what about this injection or pinprick cut?" asked Lissa.

"Coincidental. Something done prior to death."

I ran a finger over the tiny wound. "You sure, Petrie?"

"Yes, Captain. Cause of death is anoxia."

Behind me, Seb and Zac whispered over the death of *Santa Claus*. Speculation bred rumors, and I shushed them. "Can you tell me how he survived without a ship suit? Was there air in that room?"

"In some areas, oxygen was present and cycling after whatever fight left holes in the *Lucky Fish*." Petrie's eyes narrowed. "You look like you have another question."

"Yeah, which one of us killed him?" You'd have thought I'd sucked the air from our ship the way Seb gasped. "Do the math, Seb."

I couldn't see his eyes behind those enormous sunglasses he wore, nor did his mouth-flap tilt to indicate comprehension. Seb held up his hands. "There is no math to complete. I assume this is another idiom?"

The only non-Earthling on board, and he spoke better English than me. Toss him a saying, and he'd be chewing on it for the next hour. "Think about it. Victim died of...anoxia, but that room itself took no damage. Air was circulating. So how'd he die?"

Zac asked, "Airflow controller ain't on the fritz, is it?"

"Sensors would've picked up the increase throughout the ship."

"Not with all them holes, Captain." Zac frowned. "Wasn't any air to check. It'd all been sucked out."

Lissa leaned against the wall, arms crossed and eyes narrowed. "Airflow controller was one of the salvaged parts. Booted up just fine for Zac's lackey," she said.

Nick had been right. Damned fool had been destined to die in space. Not that he hadn't had it coming. He was an asshole at best and mobster at worst.

"I wonder if it was a safe room. Pretty common on passenger ships, and it would explain why the room had its own circulation system," said Lissa.

"Maybe this Santa felt all dizzy or something from CO buildup. Messed up and took the wrong drugs? Maybe he went and shot himself up with something that later killed him? Something that interacted with CO levels?" Jake asked.

An interesting idea, but I shook my head.

"Captain?"

I wrested my glance from the stiff.

"Mr. Johnson received a dose of adrenaline sometime before death. If it had been fatal, his heart muscles would display signs of stress, of pumping harder," Petrie explained. "His blood work would show the increase of adrenaline or the chemicals found in whatever drug he could've taken, but nothing showed up in my preliminary tests. The dose he received was too small to do much of anything. Certainly not kill him."

I tapped my gold sliver of a wristband. "Bridge." Once connected I asked, "Did our sensors pick up any trace signatures when we approached the *Lucky Fish*? Like someone leaving as we arrived?"

The crew member on duty answered in the negative, then asked, "Would you like me to run a second analysis of the scans to be sure?"

"Yes, and send the report to my inbox." To my officers, I said, "Maybe the injection was a trick. Something to make us look the other way or ignore his death altogether."

My crew stared at each other, taking turns to weigh suspicions and prejudices. It was comical in a way, made more so by the stripes of pungent cinnamon paste under their noses.

The wall display read 21:04. A long day that would only get longer if I was gonna figure out who knocked off Nick. "Zac and Seb, I want a complete report on the airflow controller and any other parts on the *Lucky Fish* that might explain this. Petrie, run your tests, and Lissa, start looking into what crew may or may not have had ties with our victim. We'll meet at 02:00 in the common area."

Five people I trusted stood around a dead myth until Petrie zipped the mesh bag closed. My officers left the room individually--none of them wishing to turn their back on another.

Not that I blamed them.

Alone with the doc, I said, "Petrie-Dish, I don't want to jump to any conclusions, but I think someone from my crew killed him."

With a glance at the emptying hallway, she leaned close to my ear. "Don't tell a single one of them what I'm going to say, but I agree. You were on the *Lucky Fish* for twenty minutes before we found Mr. Johnson. Based on the body's lack of lividity, he was deceased for approximately ten minutes when Seb found him. He died right under our noses."

"The room was sealed until one of us pried it open, Petrie. It had its own air circulation, but someone tinkered with it."

She wrinkled her nose, but not at any smell in the infirmary. "Then we're all suspects at this point. Someone did something to cause the buildup of carbon monoxide. Question is, was it intentional? I'll run more tests."

She slid the metal tray bearing Nick into the wall and closed the door. The unit locked with a beep after she pressed her hand to the frontal display screen. "Captain, don't take this the wrong way, but something odd did show up in my autopsy."

I tilted my head but said nothing.

"I ran a print scan, and this Nick Johnson, he doesn't exist. There is no record on file."

I allowed the breath I'd been holding to seep out in a slow exhale. "He must be a criminal then. Any record of such things?"

"Captain, when I say there's no record, I mean it. He's a ghost." The stringent odor of antiseptics hit me as she lathered her arms up to the elbow. "I'll run DNA, but that will take time."

My insides trembled. "Keep digging," I said and fled the infirmary.

Once in my quarters, I leaned against the door as my body shook. I wasn't certain why I was hiding Nick's identity; whether it was for his good or my own, I couldn't be sure, but they couldn't know.

They didn't need to know because I didn't kill my father.

I dug through a wall-drawer for a tattered box hidden in the back. I wrestled it from beneath a pair of old boots and set it on my desk. At first, I merely stared at it, but as the silence settled around me like his red cloak, I lifted the lid off the memories.

Nick's face stared at me from the digital photo, his cheeks pink from the mountain's snow. What began as a sigh left me curled in a ball like a child.

I didn't love him--hell, I didn't know him--but now I never would.

I HADN'T MEANT to doze.

The report on the *Lucky Fish*'s circulation system confirmed that the air system was fully operational up until the time of death. Someone from my crew had to have tampered with it. After reading this and grinding my teeth at the implications, I'd dozed until something woke me.

A door rattle wasn't normally the type of noise I'd notice, but my sleep had been uneasy and light. Dreams about the day Nick had left, and Gran shouting at him and cursing his name. Seeing her again, even in dreams, left me brittle.

The bleary wall-clock struck midnight, and thumping footfalls paused outside then continued on.

The door panel glowed blue at my approach. "Display heat sources in corridor A," I whispered. One figure moved toward the common area. It wasn't unusual to see folks moving about, but something in my gut told me to follow. The door hissed open as I left my quarters in pursuit.

The creeping figure ahead wore all black and carried a sack tossed over its shoulder. The overhead lights, dimmed for nighttime, cast jagged shadows, and I cursed the lack of foresight that left me weaponless. A door ten feet ahead opened and closed in rapid succession.

When I approached, the door slid open a second time, bathing me in light. Too much light for the common area. Rather than their normal white, the overhead lights twinkled in reds and golds to the rhythm of an odd thump, and I held up a hand to block the glare. "What in all hells--"

"My apologies, Captain. I was testing their luminosity. Allow me to decrease the illumination." Seb's hairless eyebrows danced above heavily darkened lenses the size of my fist. He dropped the bag on the table before he set about adjusting the lights on a handheld control screen.

"Seb, I don't mean you any insult, but what in the world are you doing in here carrying--" I riffled through the bag. "--A bag of socks?"

He slid a sealed box of thumbtacks across the table. "Once I completed my report on the airflow controller, I researched the mythos of Santa Claus. With one of his servants on board, I thought it might help us through our turmoil if we carried on with our own good cheer."

"Good cheer? During a murder? What are you talking about, Seb? That man isn't Santa--"

He shook out the lengthier socks before tacking them to the wall above the baseboard ventilation shaft. "Captain, I am aware of these facts, but we have a murderer among us. That is not something I wish to dwell on. Instead, I will hang these stockings by the chimney with care--"

"Stop." Another sock dangled between his fingers, this one bearing blue and green stripes, and I asked, "Why are you nailing socks to my ship's walls?"

"In the mythos of Earth's Christmas, Earthlings suspended stockings from chimneys in order to summon the great Saint Nicholas. Also, it is possible they protect against dust bunnies. Are dust bunnies a common fear among Earthlings?"

He hung two more socks on the wall, and I shook my head. "You realize he's a myth, right? Santa Claus isn't real. Neither are dust bunnies for that matter."

Seb continued his "decorating" until ten socks hung from the wall--one for each of my crew--though one sock dangled half the length of the others.

"What's with the short one?" I asked.

"Have you ever heard of *gherblins*?" I shook my head. "Sometimes *gherblins* creep onto the ship at night and steal the socks my mother knits. When my socks no longer possess a mate, I stow them in a box to send home."

"So what? You shrank one?"

Seb shook his head. "After we ferried that group from Yabanc last year, someone left the miniature stocking in the cargo bay. I suspect one of their offspring may have mislaid it."

He slung the empty bag across his shoulder. His mouth-flap split, both top lips forming a half-grin. Coupled with his sunglasses and unusually pale skin, it painted a grotesque picture. My skin crawled like I'd walked through a cobweb. "Is there anything else you require, Captain?" Seb asked.

I wanted to tell him, explain why I was bothering with Nick. I mean, he was my first mate. I should've been able to trust him. Instead, I shrugged it off. "I hate complications."

"That is completely understandable." Seb turned away from the door frame as he continued to decorate.

"Someone killed that man, and I gotta ask, Seb, why do this in the middle of the night? Did it ever occur to you that I might've thought you the murderer? Might still?"

His bushy orange wig escaped his hood when he laughed. "Me? Kill Santa? I am not the one experienced in dead bodies."

"Petrie? Why suspect her?"

"Why not? We are all capable of horrible deeds, are we not? Even you, I suspect."

Yes, I am.

He mistook my silence and said, "No offense intended, Captain." As he sauntered from the room, fro first, I remained alone with blinking lights and empty stockings, both of which chased my thoughts in circles. Petrie had been on my ship during the murder, or so I'd thought. Besides, no way a woman like her would know a crook like Nick, much less have a reason to kill him. Or so I thought.

As much as I didn't want to admit it, Petrie *did* have access to all manner of medicines and the knowledge to cover up the crime. It wouldn't be the first time Nick had steered a new crew member my way in order to set me up. It was time to find out what Ol' Nick had been up to in the years since I'd last seen him.

I swore as I trudged back to my quarters. Nothing good would come of this business with Ol' Saint Nick.

But then, nothing ever had.

THE SECTOR'S trace report noted no fewer than five ships in the area before our arrival, but none of them during Nick's murder. Just my ship, *The Perffaith*. Without access to the *Lucky Fish*'s computer, a spacewalk in a black hole would've been easier than tracing Nick's movements. Zac could've helped, being my local computer expert, but at this point, I didn't trust anyone.

Sad truth was, I wanted to trust them all.

The last time I'd seen Nick, he'd been on Europa running "errands" for Junto, the father of Europa's crime family. I pecked at the handheld screen, which glared in the darkness until I swiped a finger down the side to dim it. A search of his name pulled up a list of warrants, arrest records, and bounties. His current address showed up as unknown. Not exactly surprising, especially if he were still working for Junto.

We'd last met in his shack on Europa. Too much condensation and not enough filtration had left the walls a pattern of black and green splotches, and my nose twitched at the memory. The business card he'd given me that day--*Raymond Royant, Antiquities Dealer*--had a relay code which I now keyed in. Error messages scrolled across the screen.

"No such contact. Would you like to execute a last known trace-run?"

I hit the "no" button and leaned my head against the wall. How do you find a guy who lives off the grid?

A green light blinked on my handheld. "Incoming Call--Unknown Number."

"Accept call," I said. No picture appeared--just an empty, black screen.

"Whosit?" a gruff voice asked.

"Since you called, you tell me. By any chance, is this Raymond--"

"I asked you a question, boy. Whosit?"

I cleared my throat. "Um, this is Mark Banes. If this is Raymond, I met you once with Nick--"

The black screen fizzled a moment until Raymond's grumpy face appeared. If I hadn't known any better, I'd have sworn he'd been wearing that same flannel shirt when I'd met him a few years back. Bloodshot eyes glared at me above a week's worth of stubble. He sat cross-legged in some shack whose walls were lined with cardboard, and he smacked his screen when it grew fuzzy. "I get ya. Yer that turd who left yer dad when he's all sick and shit. Rat bastard's who ya are."

I rolled my eyes visibly, even for a bad connection. "Look, I'm not here to argue his merits or lack of them with you. I just wanna know where he is." I knew the answer, but I was hoping that lying would get me a trail of where he'd been.

"Nick left."

"When?"

"I dunno. Do I look like his secretary? Damn bitch was hot, too. Hotter than me." Raymond took a swig from a bottle he'd been storing between his knees. "Yer hair's shorter than that time you visited Nick."

I ran a hand over my brown head. "He still working for Junto?"

Raymond flinched but nodded. The screen flickered then went dark, and the dissonant tritone of a disconnect assaulted my ears.

The last time I'd seen my father, he'd given me some song and dance about being terminal. It wasn't the first time I'd heard that line of bull. Nick's one skill was looking out for number one--that was him. Whether he'd owed Junto's boys money or had bought into some get-rich-quick-scheme, he'd come running to Gran and me when he was low on cash. Or booze. Or both.

And I'd run just a little bit further into space and away from him.

I thought I'd run far enough. Seems as though he'd found a way to run to me.

NICK'S DEATH, the reality that he'd had cancer, and my lack of sleep left me with visions of drunken bums dancing in my head like a bad 3D flick while I contemplated calling Junto. I had a good hour before the 02:00 meeting with the crew. With a heavy sigh, I put in the call to the Callisto Space Station.

I'd repeated my request to five lackeys before I reached someone physically stationed on Europa, then to another lackey before reaching the Family proper. "I know you don't wanna tick off your boss, but see, he owes me one," I said to the funny little man on my screen. His mustache--if one could call a pencil-thin line scribbled above one's upper lip an actual mustache--twitched. "Tell him Captain Mark Banes would like to call in a favor."

The screen went a hazy, snowy gray for another minute or two before the man himself appeared. He'd lost a good fifty pounds since I'd last seen him, and his comb-over was more wilt than comb. I grinned like we were old friends. "How's life in the Family, Junto? You're looking good."

He didn't return my smile but wagged a thin finger at me. "Where is he?"

"Where's who?"

Junto leaned so close to his screen that his nose near bumped against it. "Your father, who do ya think? Son-of-a-bitch nicked some priceless antiquities from...a client. He was s'posed to deliver them to me, but he got all chicky. Took off with the goods."

"Nick's anything but a coward." My left eye twitched, and I tried to ignore it.

"There's somethin' you ain't tellin' me. Now I know I owe you a favor, which I'm willing to make good on, but I can't help you if you're lyin' to me."

"Let me guess. This is what he stole." I held up the snow globe. This time, his nose touched his screen, and I got a shot of more nose hairs than I needed.

"Where is he? Don't make me--"

"He's dead."

Junto's lips tilted up at the corners.

So he already knew that, did he? I continued fishing. "Found him dead on a beat-up ship out here in the Theros cluster. What was Nick doing on the *Lucky Fish*?"

"I assume hidin' from me."

"And it's just a coincidence that I happened upon him?"

Junto leaned away from the screen for a moment of whispering with some shadow in the background before he returned. "Look Mark, I'll tell you what I know, because we're...friends, but after this we're square. I won't owe you shit. Got it?"

It wasn't a fair trade, and the rat bastard knew it. "Fine. Tell me everything."

"Normally Nick made good on his deals, one way or another, but sometimes he gots to thinkin' he could skip the middle man. Took off with that globe-thingy you got, some honest-to-god books--"

I cut him off. "I mean no offense, Junto, but I already know what he took. Get to the bit about him being all corpsified on the *Lucky Fish*."

Junto's eyes narrowed. "My sources say he'd fooled that captain into thinkin' he was more than some two-credit con artist." He waited for me to react, and when I merely shrugged, he asked, "What? No love for *honest* Nick?"

"Say what you want. He *was* a con man. I've got no warm fuzzies for him."

"Raymond's right. You're quite the bastard. I like it!" Junto laughed with his arms wrapped around a much smaller gut. "Once I found his hidin' spot, I sent some of my boys to recover the goods."

"You sure that was all they were there to do?"

"If I wanted Nick dead, there's all manner of folks I coulda sent. I wanted the loot. That's it."

I shook the snow globe before the screen. "I assume the goods are valuable. Why'd your boys leave without them?"

"Fool captain of the *Lucky Fish* believed Nick. Can you imagine? Thought your old man was some freakin' saint or some shit. Captain refused to give me what I was owed, so my boys got...messy. Ship was in pieces when they boarded. Weren't any trace of Nick or the goods."

"You didn't look very hard."

Junto smiled into the screen. "You know everything I do."

He was lying. If he'd wanted the goods, he'd have taken them. Or asked me to fetch them seeing how I was holding them. I wouldn't push a man like Junto too hard--doing so would only result in my death if I were lucky, and the deaths of my entire crew if I were not--but I could certainly play a little.

"Seeing as how you've gone and lost your goods, what's in it for me to return them? I could part--"

Junto severed the connection before I'd finished. While I had the *why* to Nick's appearance on the *Lucky Fish*, it didn't tell me who had killed him or their reasoning. Junto's boys had been long gone by the time Nick had asphyxiated.

I swiped a hand across my screen to lock it. I'd hoped it would be unnecessary, but maybe the search among my crew would yield more answers. At a minimum, we'd start with interviews.

I hoped my crew was in a truthful mood.

BEFORE I COULD SHADOW my eyes from the twinkling lights, Lissa's pile of braids blocked the brightness. "Morning, Captain." She resumed her pacing while she gestured towards the seat awaiting me.

The rest of my crew straddled benches along either side of the table.

Bags drooped beneath most eyes, and no one paid any mind to the socks tacked to the back wall.

"It's not even 02:00 yet," I muttered and hooked a stool leg with my foot. When it scraped across the floor, Seb flinched and sent a splash of red sludge over his mug's rim. "Everyone's a mite jumpy this early morning."

Lissa cleared her throat. "Not surprising given the circumstances and lack of sleep."

"Fair enough. I did a little digging about our corpse. Seems he had a run in with Junto and the Family."

"Our stiff was a mobster? Cool." Jake threw up his hands at my glare. "Or not cool. Shame on him. Bad Mr. Santa Mobster."

I rapped my knuckles on the table. "Enough. Junto's boys were long gone when we arrived, so they weren't the killers. Someone on *my* ship murdered Sant--I mean, Mr. Johnson. Maybe it was self-defense. Maybe it was spur of the moment or even an accident. Either way, we got a corpse on our hands and not a whole lotta answers."

"Are we sure it was one of us?" Lissa asked, and I nodded.

"Analysis says we were the only ship within three hours of the *Lucky Fish* at the time of death. Someone on *The Perffaith* killed him. I want everyone interviewed, Lissa. Where they were, what they were doing-- report to me by noon."

"There is not any need, Captain." When Seb stood, his eyes hiding behind oval frames, my gut played a round of slug-it-out with my esophagus. "I think we know who our killer is."

Many feet shuffled beneath the table. "Considering we don't have much more than a mob connection and an autopsy, I find that surprising, Seb."

Zac whispered, "The autopsy. It would be easy to--"

"To what? Lie? Break my oath? Is that what you're suggesting?" asked Petrie. Her end of the bench slid sideways as she rose to her feet. When she leaned across the table toward Zac, Lissa's hand on my arm stopped my own forward motion.

"Might as well see what shakes loose. This has been brewing all morning," Lissa said.

Without so much as a glance in our direction, Seb said, "Peter, I--"

"It's pronounced Pe-tree, not Pe-ter."

"Petrie then. You cannot deny how easy it would be for you to doctor an autopsy. You have access to needles and medicines we do not, and--"

For all her plain looks, Petrie's height made for an imposing figure as she leaned close enough to kiss Seb. The tips of her shoulder length hair bounced off his chin, and he flushed to match the blinking red lights. "Why would I risk my career to kill a stranger?"

"It is not my business to say."

"Don't think I don't know, Seb."

She broke eye contact when I knocked my fist on the table. "Enough double-speak. If you know something, either of you, get to it. Otherwise, sit down and shut up. We've got better ways to spend our time."

"Seb's been spying on me. Late at night when he thinks no one's watching," said Petrie, and Seb hissed.

"Why would he do that?" I asked.

Lissa, who had been calm a moment before, paled. Petrie reached out to grip Lissa's shoulder. "Lissa and I are together. A couple. *Alphans* are not known for their tolerance of...well..."

I closed my eyes. Onboard relationships--damned things never ended well. At best they fizzled out, and at worst, they burned a hole through the ship. A picture of the *Lucky Fish*'s bridge came to mind.

Beside me, Lissa was a confident woman who wore her strength physically as well as mentally. My chief medical officer--Petrie-Dish Extraordinaire as I called her--was an old friend but the complete antithesis of Lissa. Petrie embraced her curves like she had middle age, with shy apologies. The idea of Lissa hooking up with someone suffering under insecurities made little sense to me.

But then, nothing about the past twelve hours made any sense.

Petrie bit her lip as she awaited my response.

"As a general rule, I dislike onboard relationships. However, I see no reason for concern here. What Petrie and Lissa do in their spare time is their own business," I said.

Seb's shoulders slumped forward as Petrie turned away from him. If his mouth-flap could've frowned, it would've. Lissa kept herself angled between him and Petrie, and her finger brushed the taser clipped to her belt.

"Lissa will interview folks, then I'll interview her. She'll send me the reports by noon."

"I'd suggest we search rooms as well," said Lissa.

I waved a hand at her. We weren't there--*yet*. There had to be an easier explanation to this than murder.

"And who gets to interview you, Mark?" asked Zac.

It was Lissa who answered. "I will."

"But what if you two are in cahoots? I hate to suggest it, but if we're all suspects, we're *all* suspects. Besides, you two have a somewhat colorful past."

Zac was right. I hated when he was right. I rubbed my temples and answered, "You can all interview me. Fair?"

"Whatever you say, Captain."

The edge to his voice confused me. I glanced around the table only to be met by furrowed brows and deep frowns. Trouble was brewing like a solar flare. Whatever was happening, I was gonna have to deal with it quickly.

THE SECOND RUN of *The Perffaith*'s sensors showed the majority of my crew on the *Lucky Fish* as they should've been, the exceptions being Zac and Petrie. Sensors indicated both had left *The Perffaith* when Seb had spotted the heat source. That aside, I awaited the rest of the reports with a spinning mind and stomach.

Another blip--this one from Petrie--pinged my inbox before noon. I don't know what I'd expected the medical report to tell me beyond what I already knew--carbon monoxide poisoning, adrenaline injection, blah-blah medical jargon--but her write-up gave an alarmingly accurate portrayal of Nick's life. I reread the last paragraph twice to be sure I'd gotten it right.

Liver cirrhosis indicates a heavy drinker. Scarring of the lungs and esophageal tissue indicates heavy tobacco use. No indications of drug use in the blood or tissue. Five cysts, 2 cm. in size, were removed from the lungs, and two 1 cm cysts were removed left of the trachea. Tests revealed these cysts to be malignant in nature. Patient probably suffered from Stage IV lung cancer at the time of death. No evidence of standard or unusual cancer treatment (radiation, stem cell placement, etc.) was found.

Damn. My old man hadn't been lying after all. I closed the report and put in a call to Zac.

He stood beside a pile of scanners, their motherboards spread out across the table. "Whatcha need, Captain?"

"Meet me in the captain's station in five minutes."

He nodded as I closed the call and left my room. As I walked to the bridge I passed Jake, who stared at his shoes. No one on the bridge paid me any mind. Once the door to the captain's station slid shut, I settled in behind my desk and pulled up my recent research.

"Officer Zac Curtis requests entry," the computer announced a few moments later.

"Approve."

The door slid open, and Zac stepped inside. "I figured you'd call me down sooner or later." When I cocked an eyebrow, he added, "I've done all I can to try and salvage the *Lucky Fish*'s computer, but the data's too dang damaged--"

"That's not why I called you here."

I tapped the screen beside me and angled it to give him a better view. The picture of Nick and me was old, but it didn't take Zac longer than an exhale to make the connection.

His mouth fell open, then closed, and then opened again. "I assume you plan on telling me why you went and took a picture with Santa?"

I nodded. "You remember a few years back when my old man sent me a message saying he was dying?"

"Yeah, but--wait, *that* Nick is *this* Nick?" He squinted at the screen. "Whoa. Last time I saw his raggedy ass we were both still kids and your Gran was tossing him out for drinking again. When'd he get so old?"

I closed the image with a shrug. "Years bouncing from place to place, doing odd jobs for Junto and his boys will age someone quick enough." I pulled up Petrie's autopsy report. "Petrie says he was dying. Cancer."

Zac let out a low whistle. "So he wasn't scamming you last time, huh?"

"Apparently not. Though it doesn't explain who killed him."

"Or why you're keeping this info secret from everyone," said Zac.

"What happened between me and Nick in the past...is personal, and you'll keep this information to yourself for the time being. It'll only make waves, and the last thing we need is more tension."

Zac nodded, but his fingers toyed with the buttons on his shirt. "You know they'll think it's you. Especially if they discover the damage between you two."

I pulled up the last email I'd received from Nick. "I can't help that. It wasn't me--I've got no reason to kill him."

"Except that he abandoned you and your ma, and later your Gran. Hell, left your Gran with quite the debt if I recall. Then he left you with nothing more than a dream of what a dad's s'posed to be. Sounds like a pretty damned good reason to me."

Zac scanned the email on the screen. "You went to see him?" When I nodded, Zac asked, "Why?"

"Curiosity mainly. You know me well enough to know that I wouldn't kill him, no matter how much I hated him. The others don't. Especially Seb. He's new to the crew and wouldn't understand."

I didn't imagine the scowl on Zac's face, but like a flickering screen it blinked away a second later. "Why'd you go and pick him up, anyway? Nothing against his people, but it's uncanny the way he looks at us. Like we're dinner."

Another report scrolled across my screen. This one an addendum from Lissa on which crew had kin ties to the Europan Family. Only one name popped up, an engineer in Zac's department whose great-great-great grandmother married an ex-mobster. The details blurred before my eyes. "Junto."

"You took on that freak for your first mate for Junto?" Rather than his usual laughter, Zac's nostrils flared slightly.

"He arranged for some of the more...lucrative jobs to come our way in exchange for my accepting Seb on board as first mate. It's complicated, and we needed the cash. What can you tell me about Jelgins?" I asked.

"Engineer?" Zac rubbed his jaw. "Seems stable enough. Why? Peg him for the murderer or something?"

"Lissa found a tie with the Family--"

"His great-something-or-other, right?" Zac snorted. "He's no more a mobster than I am. Though Seb, you know he's reporting back to Junto."

I closed the report without responding to his comment. "I need you to hack into Nick's email account."

"What email client does he use?"

"M-net."

"Of course. It's free. Shouldn't be too hard."

My best friend tapped a few buttons and once at the client, he clicked the login button and typed a long word into the password field. One keystroke later, Nick's email scrolled across the screen.

"Easy password."

"That *was* easy. What was it?"

He rolled his eyes at me. "Your full name."

ZAC LEFT me alone with the emails and my thoughts, neither of which were any good. The man had barely said more than a dozen words to me (when he wasn't asking for money that was), but had used my name for his password. It left me unsettled as I crawled through messages from Junto and his boys. The majority were little more than an address and a date and time. Damned fool didn't delete anything. Must've driven Junto crazy with all his rules on security and traceability.

Three screens in had gotten me nowhere. Rather than spin my wheels on mob business, I pulled up a search to compare Nick's account with the names and email addresses of my crew. The computer made short work of my search, and the name that popped up wasn't the name I'd expected.

Over a dozen messages linked Lissa to my father, the earliest made two years prior. The first inquired about the murder of Melinda Mathis-Kerric. I made a note to look into it and kept reading. Lissa's emails to my father grew more insistent, first a short inquiry and when Nick revealed his usual non-caring self, she pointed fingers at Junto, the mob, and finally Nick.

The last message asked to meet, and the date lined up with some vacation time Lissa had taken a few months back. Nothing further appeared in the search, and I typed in a request for emails to Junto on the same date. One result appeared.

Received: by 10.93.34.126.43.122 with SSIMTP id 3927be492; Saturday, February 8, 2106 03:45:21 (-7 Standard Time) Content-Transfer-Encoding: ProxyBit.
TO: J3984@i.mw.mail.com
FROM: NickyYB@e.mw.mnet
SUB: Melinda

MESSAGE: Just so we're crystal, I don't plan to tell her nothing about the hit. Ain't like she's Family. So get your head out of your ass about this. I got it.

MY SEARCH on Melinda turned up dozens of articles. The laser gun used and the way her body had been tossed into the black to drift pointed to a mob hit, but police found little to link her to the Family. She'd once dated one of Junto's boys, but when she'd discovered his ties, she'd broken it off. The obituary had been brief and lacking emotion, and I skimmed through it until I reached the final line:

Melinda Mathis-Kerric is survived by her husband, Clay; her sister-in-law, Lissa Kerric; and her two children.

I tagged the pages and saved them in a folder. Not only did Lissa have the ability to take out someone like Nick, she had motive as well.

Dammit, why'd she always have to complicate everything?

WHEN THE DOOR slid open to the common area, my crew awaited their turn with a galaxy between each of them. No one talked. No one shared stories about Lissa kicking the ass of some thief or Zac getting *The Perffaith* to limp along on half-baked goods 'til we hit a repair station. The only people touching were Lissa and Petrie, who held hands under the table.

"I ran a search on everyone's email accounts." Minor reactions to my statement: Lissa's jaw clenched, Zac nodded to himself, and Seb's shoulders slumped. But it was Petrie who surprised me as she bit her lip. "I know where everyone was supposed to be when we searched the *Lucky Fish* and where they said they were, but I want to hear it for myself. We'll start with Jake."

He answered as soon as I finished his name. "Was on the bridge with you, Captain."

"The entire time?" asked Lissa.

"I followed the Captain to the engine room once Zac let up a shout. Never left the Captain's side."

Zac held up a finger. "Wait, aren't you gonna tell us what you found in your search? I mean, you--"

He stopped when I gave the slight shake of my head. For the moment, the fewer who knew about my crawling into Nick's past the better. Besides, everyone but Lissa had come up clean. She was no Petrie, no jumpy woman who hid behind frumpy clothing and a microscope. Lissa didn't use her physical appearance as some women might either. Her cargo pants weren't too tight, nor was her button-up shirt undone in some lame attempt to sway opinion. Nor did she lean across the table in my direction. Instead, she leveled her gaze on me--relaxation to a T. Had she been this calm when meeting with Nick over her sister-in-law's murder?

"The data search through user accounts didn't pay off. Nothing beyond the typical came up: porn, family correspondence, the regular. Lissa, retrace your steps for me," I said. A small lie but a necessary one.

"Until Seb spoke of trouble, I was standing guard outside the engine room as requested. No crew left until I escorted them back to *The Perffaith* on your orders."

"You stood outside the doors, not inside?"

"Yes, Captain."

Did you ever leave your post? Did anyone else see you there?

She must've followed along the same thought trail as she shook her head. "No one passed by until you arrived, so no one can verify my whereabouts."

A red light dangling from the ceiling blinked once more before going dark, and my officers glanced up at the sudden light shift.

"Okay, I know this is an important convo and all, but what the hell is all this crap? Besides distracting?" Zac asked as he pointed at the stained child's sock on the wall.

"I had attempted to encourage cheer through the use of items from the mythos of Saint Nicholas," whispered Seb.

Zac held the short sock up by its end. "Yeah, but what's up with the halfling stocking?"

His laughter pulled up short as Lissa spoke. "That must be yours, Zac. See? It's short like your temper."

Zac's face froze as he clenched his jaw. What used to be jokes between my crew, now caused tension. Something had broken in our group, and a few minutes' laughter wasn't gonna heal it.

The last thing I needed was a fight, so I returned to the topic at hand. "Zac, why were you coming from the cargo hold when Seb mentioned trouble?"

"I wanted to check on little Seb first. Make sure he wasn't in any trouble, being new and all and most likely to get killed walking up the stairs." Zac slapped Seb on the back.

Seb's sunglasses slid down his nose, and he winced from the lights before shoving the thick glasses back into place.

I would've said he met my gaze, but with his eyes hiding behind his sunglasses, I would've never known. Always hidden--everything about him. He didn't flinch or scowl either like I would've at Zac's ribbing. Calm as I'd never been--not since before we'd found Nick's corpse.

"He would not have discovered me in the cargo hold as I was already seeking our heat source. The cargo bay bore an enormous hole in its hull. A single crate remained, anchored to the wall. After the scanners began working, I followed the blip."

"Did anyone see you?" asked Petrie.

He shook his head. "Not until I encountered Jake and Zac."

"And you, Zac?" I asked. "Seems to me I ordered you to remain on board *The Perffaith*."

"Ain't no way I did it. By the time I got on the *Lucky Fish* and got the heat source all sorted out, I would've had no time to reach our vic," said Zac.

I shrugged. "That leaves you, Petrie-Dish."

"I was on board *The Perffaith* until Seb mentioned the corpse."

"Where on *The Perffaith*?" asked Seb. He was standing again, his mouth-flap curled back and open. "Can anyone confirm your precise location?"

"The computer can," answered Zac. "The logs show the correct time stamp for when she left Lissa's room for the *Lucky Fish*."

Interesting. She hadn't been in the infirmary, and Zac had known it. Why'd he been digging through the logs? Seb halted his pacing to glare at Petrie.

Lissa rose when Seb stepped in Petrie's direction--a swift motion I caught out of the corner of my eye. She placed both hands on Seb's shoulders. Lissa towered over Seb and glanced down her nose to see past his shades. "If you've got a problem with Petrie's personal life, get over it. Look at her or anyone else on this ship like that again, and it won't matter that you're first mate. I'll pitch you out the ship myself," she said.

He wriggled in her grasp, but she held him firmly in place. "If you would allow me go."

"Apologize."

Seb shot me a plea for help, and I shrugged. He got himself into this; he could get himself out of it.

"My apologies, Petrie. Everyone." He stumbled back when Lissa released him.

"Captain, I think it's time for that room search. It's too easy for us to cover for one another," said Lissa.

I nodded. Maybe in our search, we'd find something tying someone to Nick, someone else. Maybe I'd figure out what had happened when Lissa had met with him.

Or maybe I'd figure out why it rattled me so much to see her kicking sideways with Petrie.

PETRIE'S ROOM was first on our list, if for no other reason than to shut Seb up. Everything tucked into place, her room was nearly unlived in. Dust gathered in the bottom of a laundry hamper and across the food dispenser. Bed neatly made and floor cleared of any tripping hazards. Everything in its place, unused.

She stood, arms across her chest, as Zac and I dug through what few belongings remained in the room. At the door, Seb and Lissa watched, the latter with wide stance as she guarded the doorway.

It didn't feel right to be combing through Petrie's belongings like I was, but my hands busied themselves as my mind wandered.

I almost didn't catch it, so buried was it in a wadded up shirt shoved into an otherwise empty drawer. When my fingers closed around the hard object, I sighed.

"What is it?" Zac whispered, and I opened my palm to display a capped needle.

"Safety ring's missing. I assume it's used, though it's hard to say if it was used on Santa."

In a room the size of a small shuttle, whispers carried like a baby crying. By the look on Petrie's face, she'd heard it all.

"The needle's mine, though it wasn't used on our Santa." Petrie pulled out a vial from another drawer and held it up. "Allergen serum."

"For...?" I asked.

"I'm allergic to Lissa's cat."

Seb muttered something in <u>Alphan</u> as he fled the doorway.

"Run it for DNA...On second thought," I turned and handed the needle to Jake, "have her assistant run it. Send the results to me direct."

Jake left, with Petrie closely behind. Lissa stepped on my boot heels as she followed me toward Seb's room. When I reached the door panel, it read *unlocked* and the room occupied. Lissa stood opposite me, her hand on her taser.

"Be careful, Mark," she whispered, and I arched one eyebrow. "He's been...Petrie wasn't lying when she said he's been following us. Something's off about him."

"Don't tell me you believe all that prejudicial horseshit about <u>Alphans</u>?"

"I know you don't want to hear this, but it's true. Seb believes...." She trailed off and stared at the taser in her hands. "He believes that Petrie and I are *taurists*. Evil."

I scanned the band on my wrist to announce us. "You're right, I don't want to hear about your paranoia." The same old shit as before, only it was Seb this time instead of Zac. Here I'd thought she'd changed in the past few years. "I expect you to do your job without prejudice, Lissa."

The door slid open with a faint chime. A musty odor itched my nose something fierce as I stepped inside the dark room. Seb's faint shape sat across from the door, his hand shading his exposed eyes from the hallway light. "If you do not mind, please close the door until I have my glasses," he said.

At my nod, Lissa stepped inside and allowed the door to slide shut. We stood in near pitch darkness as Seb rummaged around to my right. A slight hiss closed a metal drawer. When the lights rose, Seb leaned against the wall donning his shades. "Please feel free to search my personal belongings. There is nothing here I wish to hide."

As I approached the wall-drawers, my nose flared at the pungent odor--like sweaty socks in a microwave. No stains along the walls, so he hadn't set any biohazard growing in my ship. The odor was definitely inside a drawer, whatever it was.

I tugged a drawer open at random, and the stench of sweat and something sour bowled over me. Lissa passed me a pair of rubber gloves, and I nodded my thanks.

Nothing hid within the "clean" laundry, but nestled inside the corner desk were three journals, each held together with a sinew-type thread down the middle.

"Please do be careful with those." His voice cracked as he spoke.

"Is that leather? Or...something else?" asked Lissa.

Touching their covers was not in my plan. No telling what skin they came from. Lissa picked one up at random, and I muttered, "I didn't know anyone still wrote on paper. If that's even paper."

Seb bobbed his head up and down. "My mother bound these

journals from the hide of a <u>whonta</u> on the day of my birth. The inside pages are from the mighty <u>rew</u> tree, which stands thirty meters in height. These books will tell my life story to my offspring and their offspring."

After a few page turns, Lissa handed me a book and pointed.

03/1/2108 21:54 PM

She has remained another evening with the security officer. They carry on, right under the captain's nose, as if it would not hurt him to see his <u>amhon</u> with another. It would crush him.

How could she remain with the security officer? To be <u>taurists</u> is unforgiveable, yet she is the moon. How can I see her as such?

Is she unaware that I stood outside for ten minutes? Did I perhaps misjudge her invitation to stop by and discuss current medicinal treatments for the itching of the scalp? Perhaps she meant for me to come by another time. I must have misunderstood. She would not make such an error.

03/2/2108 09:20 AM

I cannot sleep. What am I to do? How can I love something so vile? My mother would be ashamed.

The surveillance dated back months, though his feelings were a more recent development. I snagged the other journals. Looks like I had a little light reading to do tonight.

"Will those be returned?" he asked.

"Once I've taken a look at them."

"Captain," he said, and his shades slid down his nose an inch to expose damp, dark eyes near the size of my fist. "Those--those are personal."

"So was this murder."

My wristband beeped. The DNA results were back on Nick and the needle. I swallowed hard.

"Something up?" Lissa asked.

"Later."

Other than the journals, our search of Seb's room came up empty.

The *Alphan* lived an odorous and bizarre life but had nothing connecting him to Nick. Lissa's jaw clenched as we left Seb's room.

"What is it?" I asked.

"I didn't realize...I thought--"

"You thought it was something else, not a crush that had him stalking Petrie."

She nodded. "Not that stalking isn't an issue, but oddly enough, I don't think he's our murderer. He's too much of a chicken shit. Though I suppose he could've planted that needle on Petrie."

"Nope. Tests came back. Only Petrie's DNA on the needle. It was used for her allergy shots."

"Doesn't that mean Petrie's innocent?"

I leaned against the wall with a sigh. "Not necessarily. She could've tampered with her assistant's results or even those of the autopsy. Seb's not wrong on that point."

When she shook her head, the silver beads in her braids glittered in the overhead light. It was good to see her hair long again rather than the short rainfall she'd sported before. "Maybe Seb did a botched frame job? No, it has to be someone else. Why frame someone you love?"

"Maybe because you can't have them?" I asked. The door panel outside Seb's room changed to the locked signal, and I pulled Lissa away from the door. "I tend to agree with you that he's not our guy, but I can't rule him out just yet. No more than anyone else."

She must have caught the unspoken implication as she pointed in the direction of her quarters. "Let's get this over with."

"Lissa--" I followed her down the corridor. As my security officer, her quarters were next to mine: something that had once been convenient. I bit back my question.

Her room was as I remembered it--simple and without decoration. The occasional book out of place gave the room a lived in appearance but other than that, her room was as clinical and cold as Petrie's had been. The exception was the cot, which lay in the corner beneath a mess of tussled blankets. "Tell me, Lissa. Did you kill Santa?"

"No." The light-brown hand on my forearm was pale against my dark skin. "I thought you knew me better than that, Captain."

"Why Petrie?" I cursed the wrong question that had escaped me. "Never mind, I'm not sure I care to know."

She shrugged and pulled open the wall-drawers for my perusal. I dug through her belongings and swallowed back more emotion than I cared to admit when I encountered one of Petrie's polka-dotted cardigans. "Why'd you meet with our victim, Nick?"

"What?" she asked, her hand in midair. When I didn't reply, she opened her desk drawers, all of which had been locked.

A bit of digging found most of the drawers clear of evidence, and I moved to the single shelf above her cot, which was full of trophies and awards. "You met with Nick concerning the murder of your sister-in-law, Melinda. Why?"

She folded her tall frame into the padded chair in the corner with a long sigh. "Melinda's murder was a mob hit. I knew you had contacts to the Family. I bullied Zac into giving me an email address. He gave me one for a Nick Melorrey. I thought if I talked to him, he'd be able to tell me why Junto called in a hit on her. But I never met with him, not in person."

I was gonna kill Zac for tangling her up with the Family. To Lissa, I said, "That last job with Junto went way south of normal, Lissa. You almost died. In fact, you left me after that job. What in the world would possess you to get mixed up with the Family?"

"I had to know!"

The shout caught me off guard, and I shoved a wobbling trophy back onto the shelf. Her cheeks were flushed and her eyes wide.

"The police knew it was a hit, but they refused to do anything, Mark. They said Junto was untouchable. What would you have done...if it had been me? Would you've let it go?"

No. I would've buried him with my bare hands. "Did you kill Nick?" I asked.

"No. Nick wouldn't tell my anything. He wouldn't meet with me. Just sent me useless emails full of nothing. Hell, I didn't even know our victim was *that* Nick until you mentioned the mob connection earlier."

It would've been easier if I could've believed her. "So you didn't recognize him?"

"I never saw him in person. He wouldn't accept video calls either so no. It seems our victim had many names."

I closed the last of the wall-drawers. "Room's clear."

"You believe me then?"

I spun to find her all too close. She smelled like strawberries, and I leaned forward until my nose nearly touched hers.

"Is this what you came here for, Captain?" she asked, voice colder than the *Lucky Fish.*

I flinched at the door's hiss behind me, and my nose bumped hers.

"Sorry, Captain. Didn't mean to interrupt--" I winced at Zac's words.

Behind him stood the rest of my officers. Petrie bumped into Jake's shoulder when he stopped. "Why the--" Her face crumpled.

"I apologize for suggesting it, Captain, but is it possible you have a conflict of interest?" asked Seb as he brushed past Zac. He opened the wall-drawers with less care than I'd taken. With a shrug, Zac joined him while I stood there looking the idiot. Her room turned up nothing again. Seb stepped back, stray hairs from his wig sticking to his sweaty face.

"Satisfied?" asked Lissa.

Seb stumbled away from her and tripped over a chair leg.

"Since you're convinced there's something going on, we'll do the Captain's quarters next," she said.

They expected me to lead the way. I'm not sure why I didn't, only that my brain was still arguing with my heart over what the hell had just happened. Zac led the short procession ten feet over with me trailing behind like a guilty party.

Except I wasn't.

My officers watched as Zac and Seb now searched my quarters. I took a moment to stuff Seb's journals into a wall-drawer for later reading.

When Zac and Seb reached my desk, Seb's jaw pulsed. He held up a picture frame I recognized all too well. "Why do you have a photo with Santa?" he asked, and my tongue rolled across the dry roof of my mouth. I'd forgotten to return the photo to the false bottom in the wall-drawer.

The old school digital frame was passed around the crew.

Nick had said he wanted to connect, to make up for lost time while we still had it. Rather than swallow my pride and the past, I'd shut him down. And he'd given up. I might as well have killed him myself.

"Mark?"

Damn Lissa's eyes. If they could've bored black holes through me, they would've.

"I don't know why I didn't see it before." Lissa handed Petrie the wooden frame. "Look at the nose."

"Dominant arch, flared nostrils," Petrie said. "I ran DNA on our victim, Mark. I thought it a mistake, but seeing this picture..."

Zac glanced between the digital photo and me as he shifted his weight from one foot to the other. He tried to hide his *I-told-you-so* expression behind a fake sneeze and failed.

"You knew, didn't you?" Lissa asked, and Zac studied the dirt beneath his fingernails.

I said, "Leave Zac out of this. He was following orders."

"Captain, if you have a connection to the deceased, it would be best to reveal that now." Lissa paled at Petrie's comment.

I took the photo from the doctor. "His name's not Nick Johnson. It's Nick Banes, and he's my father."

Saying the words made them real.

Feet shuffled in the room, but no one spoke. When Lissa's hand touched my shoulder, I flinched. "Mark, your father was a first grade asshole. He abandoned you. I think we'd all understand if--"

"If what?" Voice too sharp, I bit my tongue. "If I snapped and killed him? I know what this looks like, but I didn't do it. Much as I would've liked to years back, this murder wasn't me."

"How'd your father end up dead on the *Lucky Fish*?" asked Jake.

"And why were you hiding this photo?" Petrie pointed at the false bottom in the wall-drawer. "No offense, but this isn't looking good for you, Captain."

There wasn't any way I was walking out of this without being gutted. The story tumbled out too fast, too raw: his scamming first my mother, then Gran; his need for money and booze; the jobs he had done for Junto; and finally, his attempt to reconnect. "He came crawling out of the meteor field to give me some line about dying or some shit.

Wanted to get all enlightened with forgiveness at the mountain. That's when that photo was taken."

"And you decided to keep this hidden because?" asked Petrie.

"I wasn't hiding it. It's private and not relevant."

"Not relevant, my ass." Zac flushed. "Forgive me, Captain, but that's what we'd call a motive right there."

Swallowing proved difficult, yet I managed.

Petrie said, "But our victim *was* sick. The autopsy determined that."

"He was, but by the time he'd reached out to me, he'd told so many lies, killed so many...it didn't matter if he was being truthful. Either way, I didn't kill him. Jake was with me during the time of death. Are we done here?"

Zac nodded to Lissa, who announced, "Room's clean."

"Jake could be protecting you, Captain. It wouldn't be the first time someone from your crew kept you from the noose. That last job from Junto...." said Zac, and I could've strangled him. Zac threw up both hands. "Just laying out the facts...Captain."

His jaw clenched as he turned away from me.

"I didn't kill him," I said, but no one was listening.

The crew followed me from my quarters with mumbles and whispers, and my stomach churned. My crew'd gone from family to a maelstrom of accusations in less than forty-eight hours. A sweep of Jake's quarters turned up nothing more than the typical array of dirty laundry.

Lissa turned to Zac. "Where'd you get the idea to run salvage on this particular ship?" she asked.

His smile tightened at the edges. "We haven't had decent work in months. Not since...not since we took Seb on board. No one wants to deal with a vessel with an *Alphan*. Add in all that union crap--"

She waved her hand in the air. "Yes, yes, but how'd you find *this* job?"

"If we don't get more memory for the food replicators, we're gonna be eating like the junkies on Europa. When I saw this job come up on that board for folks looking for side-work, I figured it was a good fit. Ran it by Mark and off we went."

"Which board?" I asked.

I thought his lips would split, the painful way he over-grinned. "Side-Slide."

"Dammit, Zac. That site's quasi-legal at best."

"Yeah, well, it ain't like you've never taken the odd job to keep *The Perffaith* running."

Lissa sighed. "Did you know the site is backed by Junto?"

"Yes."

The answer was too fast in coming, too confident. Lissa and Zac. Both with motive. Both my friends.

"You just happened upon a salvage job within hours of a fight?" asked Lissa.

"Well, yeah."

I stared at Zac. Every lie he told poked a hole in the façade of calm demeanor. I was drowning in lies.

"While we're speaking of weirdness," said Zac as the crew walked to his room. "Lissa, how'd the meeting go with Nick?"

The procession halted. "Ya knew our stiff?" asked Jake.

Lissa sighed. "Not really. I was investigating a murder--"

"So you've done this before then?" Zac smirked.

"Dammit, shut up and let me finish. I was investigating a mob hit and needed info from someone within the Family. *Zac*--" she stressed his name, "--gave me the email address for Mark's contact, a Nick Melorrey. I didn't know it was the same man, because I never met him in person. Never even had a video chat. Just emails."

"I'm sure that's all it was," said Zac.

When this was dealt with, I was gonna have a little chat with Zac. I didn't need more shit stirred on my ship.

Zac pressed his hand to his door's panel, and the lock released. "After you, Captain," he said.

Here was another room I'd visited many a time, though usually while piss-drunk. It was the only time he'd sucker me into playing a round of poker or jack. The walls held holographic images of a dozen starships, each more decadent and expensive than *The Perffaith*. Like Petrie's room, his was neat leaning on not lived in.

I'd already skimmed each crew member's log, but I pulled up Zac's for another look while Lissa rifled through the wall-drawers. Each log noted his entrance and exit from his room, none of which were particularly suspicious until the day of Nick's murder. At 08:00, he'd left his quarters for the morning. We'd all left the infirmary at 21:04, but the computer never logged Zac as returned to his room.

All of us were desperate for sleep, and knowing Zac, he'd have caught some zee-time when he could. I scrolled down and caught this morning's log. He'd left his room at 07:30.

Zac's shadow across the screen grew in size, and I closed the file. A few clicks later had me scanning his browsing history, emails, and calls.

"Feel free to enjoy my porn collection," he said and laughed. Gaps appeared in his history--moments where he'd logged into the system and done nothing. When I didn't laugh, his reflection on the screen frowned, and I forced a grin.

Something about the lack of computer data turned my stomach something fierce. In my study of the crew's logs, dozens of lines showed their movements and computer conversations in the past two days. Zac's were mostly the same except for the holes. "Zac, when did you come back to your room last night?" I asked.

"It must have been about 23:00 or so. Just after finishing my report. Actually, make that 23:15 since Lissa interviewed me toward the tail end of things."

He'd taken the bait. Now to drag the fish along until it stopped flopping. "Something odd's going on with the computer. Between this and the scanners, I wonder "

Zac cocked his head. "Think we've been hacked or something?"

"Interesting choice of words coming from a former hacker," said Lissa. When I turned away from the computer, Lissa held Zac's scanner before her. Six heat sources read in his room. "I thought you said the scanner wasn't reading right," she said.

He shrugged. "It wasn't, but I replaced the memory this morning. Been reading just fine since then."

Lissa closed her mouth at my look. Last job we'd run had left our scanners blipping when they oughta have been blooping. Damned planetary moisture had done quite a number on their innards. I'd placed the order for new parts myself, only they hadn't arrived yet.

I didn't know why, but this was a bet I'd make sober. Zac was lying to me.

⚞

"SEEMS CONVENIENT," muttered Petrie from the doorway.

"What does?" Zac's voice was level, but he curled one hand into a half-fist.

"Your missing the heat source like that."

"Look, Petrie. I get that you're unusually gung-ho to find who killed Santa, especially if it takes the heat off of your girlfriend, but this don't mean shit. So I missed the heat source. With people blathering in their speakers at me, it's an easy mistake. Besides, Mark's dad died from CO poisoning. I still think he coulda jabbed himself with something when he felt himself go all woozy."

Seb brushed past Petrie. "Or maybe you are attempting to frame everyone for your own actions. You possess the needed knowledge to render the *Lucky Fish*'s computer silent."

"Maybe," said Zac, and he leaned nose-to-nose with Seb. "Or maybe you want it to sound that way. Since the murder, everyone's been hell-bent on accusing one another, but maybe it's just as I said. Here we are spinning our wheels over solving an accident when we could be selling our salvage. I don't know about you, Seb, but I'd like to eat something not replicated from old protein sometime this year."

Stress and lack of sleep had rendered them useless to me. I moved to step between the two, but Lissa beat me to it. "Enough," she shouted.

Before accusations started flying again, I said, "Everyone to their quarters. Let the skele-crew handle *The Perffaith*. And when I say your quarters, I mean your *own* quarters."

Petrie frowned but nodded.

"I've got to make sure the rest of the scanners are--"

I interrupted Zac with an upright hand. "I have a few leads to follow up before we finish grabbing salvage off the *Lucky Fish*. Stay in your room. Don't make me lock everyone inside."

My crew muttered as they spread out toward their quarters. Zac

104

flopped into an empty chair, his fingers already running across the screen beside him.

"When this is all done, we're gonna have a talk, Zac."

"I'm sure," he muttered.

I followed Lissa outside and sighed when Zac's door shut behind me.

"You know something," she said.

"Possibly. Feel like helping?"

Lissa grinned and led the way to my quarters. Outside my door, she turned about-face. "I'm sorry. I should've told you about Melinda--"

"Don't," I said as I opened the door with a handprint. I locked the door behind us.

On the wall screen, I put in a call to Junto. Another hold as I waited for my message to reach the proper person, and Lissa fiddled with her sealed braid tips.

"Why are you calling him?" she whispered.

The screen twitched before Junto's mug popped up. "I thought I made it clear I don't owe you."

"You did, but I needed some information."

He furrowed his brows, then a slow smile spread across his face as he glanced over my shoulder at Lissa. "I see you two have worked things out."

I dismissed his attempts to push my buttons with a shrug. "Last time we had a chat, you said your boys were here to get the goods, yet they didn't. You and I both know you sent them to knock off Nick, but you had to ensure Nick was dead in the debris. Who'd you call on my ship to be sure?"

Junto's smile didn't falter as he wrested his attention from Lissa. "What makes ya think I did any such thing?"

"No games, Junto. If you had a mole in the Fam, you'd flush him out faster than I could toss the *Lucky Fish*. Allow me to do the same."

"What will you give me for such intel?"

It was my turn to smile. "I won't mention to the authorities where to find Melinda's killer."

"You won't, anyway. You got nothin'."

I pressed a button on my screen to forward a message his way. "In a few minutes, or maybe an hour with the way relays have been delayed, you'll get an email from Nick's email account--one where he makes very sure to state that he won't meet with Lissa here or tell her what happened to Melinda. I'm sure it could link Nick and you to her, which may open more doors than you want blown open at this point. Hell, they may find the clues in their own search of your computers there on Europa." I shrugged. "But hey, if you wanna take that risk, be my guest."

Junto's left eye twitched, but he gave the slightest nod. My account pinged. Guess he had faster mail relays than me. "Don't call again."

"I don't intend to."

The screen darkened, and I pulled up the message he'd sent. The decrypted file contained a series of video messages. Whoever our killer was had disconnected the video feed and fed the voice through the computer. A robotic voice read off the details of the hit--where, when, who--not much else.

"Dammit," I muttered.

"Open another one."

Confirmation that Junto had told someone on board about the salvage and hired them to kill Nick *(if found),* but nothing more. Another file, this one giving details of a meeting between Nick and Lissa. A meeting that never happened. At least according to her.

"That...that never happened. I didn't meet with him." She curled her fingers into fists. "You have to believe me."

"I can't."

"What are you going to do?"

"Find the proof I need. One way or another." My door slid open at my approach, and I gave her a brief nudge in its direction. "Look, just head back to your room. Stay put until I figure this out."

Lissa rested her hand against my chest--a moment's warmth in the situation's chill. "Mark--"

"Don't say it. We both know you wouldn't mean it in the morning." The words were harsh, but I couldn't trust her. Not yet. I'd ask her forgiveness later, assuming I was alive to do it.

Assuming she wasn't the murderer.

My gut clenched as she left, and I pulled up the ship's map on the door panel. Heat sensors showed the two-member skeleton crew in place while the rest were in their rooms.

I sank into my cot and pressed the button to my right. A screen slid out, and I pulled up the logs from before.

The hole from last night was gone. Zac had altered his coming and goings again. The question now was why. What was he hiding now? What had I missed? I pulled up the logs from the last twenty-four hours for Lissa's rooms, but they'd been cleared as well. He'd muddied the waters.

Maybe he was protecting Lissa. Maybe they were working together.

I scrolled away from the logs and into the command panel. The computer's line to the derelict rang true enough, but the damaged ship wasn't singing back. The *Lucky Fish* ignored my request to power up. Her computer was as lifeless as my father's corpse, which shouldn't have been the case. If nothing else, she could've piggybacked off our power. The ship's black box was intact and should've been singing one last serenade.

Maybe if I brought the black box over to *The Perffaith*, I could get it talking. I grinned at my reflection in the screen.

But first, I needed to know if Lissa had met with my father. The audio mentioned a meeting at a swank hotel in Garthus. Being all hoity-toity, maybe they'd have a record.

If I'd had to pinpoint the moment when the screen grew fuzzy, I wouldn't have been able. Only that as I stared at the small screen beside me, my vision rolled with my stomach. I blinked my way through the rocking long enough to pull up the article on carbon monoxide poisoning.

Damn.

So this was how it'd been done.

THE ROOM SPUN as I staggered to the door. The killer couldn't poison the entire ship without going down with us. If I could get to the hall--
When I reached it, my door ignored my presence, and I pushed on the hand plate, which read:

LOCKED. OVERRIDE? Y/N

My finger slid across the Y, and the screen chirped a refusal. I tried to speak and couldn't. When birthdates and the names of family members didn't remove the lock, I blinked a few times while staring at the yellow glare. By the time I finished typing the L in Rachel, the world was a mix of gray haze and jagged edges. The door slid open and fresh air smacked me in the face. As I fell to my knees in the hall, I made a mental note to send the ex-girlfriend a gift of some sort. Coughs flooded the hallway as crewmembers escaped their rooms.

Jake crawled his way over to me from his room across the hall. "Need to make...sure everyone...escaped."

I nodded, but my legs refused to lift me from the floor. Weak and quivering, I reached up and slapped my hand on a nearby panel. "Head count, please," I croaked.

Eight heat sources on board *The Perffaith.* "We're missing two."

Jake said, "The murderer. And his or her accomplice?"

"It appears to be the case." This time when I tried my legs, they held, though my stomach churned. "Check that everyone's okay. I need to get to the *Lucky Fish*."

Jake took the left corridor while I went right. Coughs covered what little could be said as I passed by my crew members. The stairwell's door shut behind me, and I took the stairs two at a time. Two flights down, salvage from the *Lucky Fish* lay scattered across the cargo bay. In the airlock chamber, two spacesuits were missing.

Dammit. The killer was going for the black box. The remaining evidence.

My legs quivered as I pushed one foot and then the other through the legs of a spacesuit, and my fingers trembled against the zipper pull. Part of me wished I had help--Lissa's help, to be honest--but for all I knew, she'd kill me rather than help me.

The zipper moved easier than I did. Fitting the helmet in place was a relief as cleaner oxygen swept through it, and I inhaled deeply a few times before sealing off the chamber for depressurization.

Two seconds into the derelict, goosebumps crept across my skin. Wasn't much reason for it--my lone light split across her darkness as expected--but a slim one foot of metal between me and the dark embrace of space set my wiggins-radar to off the charts, especially being alone with one, possibly two killers.

If the killer was smart, he--or *she*--would be hiding in a twist of metal wreckage. Maybe both of them were stupid, hiding out in the bridge. The idea made my steps slow as I shined my flashlight's beam into every shadow between me and the evidence I needed.

Dead ahead, the sliding doors to the bridge remained pried open from our previous excursion. The suit's emergency knife wobbled in my hand as I leaned my head around the doorway.

Nothing. The bridge was empty.

One floating lap around the bridge confirmed what my eyes told my brain. The main panel lay open, and I used the lip to pull myself beneath it. Its innards were an enigma to me, but I had a hunch the dead panel wasn't from damage. Not directly. I reached behind a mess of wires until I brushed up against the manual power switch. It was switched on.

Beside it lay the reset button. Once flipped, the black box's display lit up. Lights blinked and error codes scrolled across the three inch screen for a full minute before the command prompt blinked twice. Waiting.

I noted the killer's entrance by the pop of my speaker and gripped my knife. I couldn't ignore the cold sweat inside my suit.

Zac held one hand behind his back. A weapon of some kind? I used the panel for leverage as I faced him. "Was it you?"

He didn't answer--his eyes focused on the black box.

"Why?" I asked, and he pushed himself through the doorway and into the bridge.

Zac held an old-fashioned gun in his hand. "Money." He jerked the weapon to the right, and the speaker in my helmet crackled. "Get away from the box."

"Or what? You'll shoot me?" My breath came too fast. If he destroyed the black box, all evidence would die with me. "You're my best friend, Zac. I can't believe you'd kill me for money."

"Quit stalling. I saw you come alone. No one's coming to save you."

A bead of sweat crawled its way across my chin. Where was Lissa? Had she worked with him? Or had she been a hostage?

"How do you know that thing will even work?" I nodded at his gun. "No oxygen on the ship."

He rolled his eyes. "See? This is why. This!" The gun jumped with his gestures. "You don't have the brains to climb out of a paper bag, yet you're the mighty captain of his own ship. How many times have I pulled your ass from the proverbial fire?"

"More times than I can count. Which is why you've got me wondering what this is all about."

My helmet's speaker crackled again with his answer. "You. Here I've gone and done everything you've ever asked of me, saved your life any number of times, nursed your broken heart after that bitch dumped you, and how do you repay me? Hmmm? By making some bigoted *Alpha*n your first officer!"

He wasn't working with Lissa? My breath caught in my throat. Then where was she? I coughed in my helmet. Oh gods. Was she dead?

"Seb was an accident. I should've never accepted him from Junto."

Zac floated within a few feet of me. Spittle decorated the interior of his helmet, and his eyes were too large for sanity. "No shit. It should've been *me*!"

I held the knife uselessly at my side. "If you had a problem with me, why go after my father?"

Over his shoulder, a light flashed once in the corridor before fading. "I told you!" he shouted, and the gun jumped closer to my faceplate. "The money. Junto was willing to pay shiploads to make sure Nick was good and dead. You weren't going to miss him and with all that money, I'd be free of *The Perffaith*."

I tried to focus on his face rather than the new shadow in the hall, but the gun sent a new round of shakes through me. For whatever reason, Zac was convinced it would fire.

I held up my hands. "You were never a prisoner here, Zac. Take your money and go."

The grin that split his thin lips was full of malice. "Can't. You know too much. How'd you figure out it was me, anyway?"

A booted foot stopped within the emergency doorway behind Zac.

The silver strip across the helmet matched those across our feet. One of my crew was here. I sighed with relief, but Zac misread my reaction.

"That's it? This is all I get from the mighty captain of *The Perffaith*? So much for being perfect. What would your precious Gran think of you now?"

Anger flushed my face. Despite the lack of gravity, my arms and legs moved too fast through the dimly lit bridge. I reached for Zac as the pistol's muzzle flashed. Something hit me and pain erupted across my ribcage.

I flipped the latches of Zac's helmet, releasing the pressure seal. His mouth opened but whatever he said was lost with the lack of oxygen.

Lissa brushed past him. When she reached me, she slapped a glob of sealant across the hole in my suit. "Can you breathe? Did the bullet penetrate?"

My helmet occluded my view of my middle. "I don't think it penetrated completely. Suit's too thick. Though I think I bruised a rib or three."

As I spoke, she held up my arm to check gauges and sensor readings. "The sealant should hold long enough to get you back on the ship, but we need to leave now."

"What about him?"

I didn't want to look at Zac. I stared at the floor while my ribcage throbbed.

"Don't look," she whispered. "We need the black box."

Lissa tugged at my arm to get me moving. "Can you access it from *The Perffaith*?"

Zac's feet drifted past my view of the floor. "Yes, now that its power is on."

We drifted through the *Lucky Fish's* dark corridors in silence. My face grew warm as fog coated the interior of my helmet. The airlock chamber stood ten feet at most, and my arm trembled as I pushed away from the wall.

"Liss..."

Her open mouth swam in the red tint of my vision, and I closed my eyes.

THE OVERHEAD LIGHT doubled in brightness, and I winced. "Somebody do somethin' about that light," I said, or I tried to say, but the first few words were more a croak than actual speech.

"Sit tight, Captain. Sip this." Petrie placed a straw against my cracked lips.

The water burned going down, yet soothed the back of my throat. This time when I opened my eyes, the light was less harsh, though my tear ducts worked overtime.

"What happened?" I asked. "Lissa--"

A hand squeezed mine, and when I turned my head, she sat beside me in the infirmary. Too many wrinkles lined her face. "The bullet didn't reach you, but it tore enough of a hole to cause problems."

"You patched it."

"Not enough. There was a pressure loss, enough that--" Her voice cracked, and she paused. "We almost lost you."

Several crew members waved at me from the view screen to my left. Petrie swiped them away and pulled up a list of numbers and diagrams. "Your blood was trying to boil its way out of your body," she said and injected something into my IV. "While the bullet didn't tear through the entire suit, you still bruised your ribs. You'll need to stay here overnight for observation. You're dehydrated and need the increased oxygen. "

"How long was I out?"

"A few hours. You came out of the hyperbaric tube half an hour ago."

Whatever she'd stuck in the line made the world prettier than I remembered, and I smiled at the fuzzy warmth.

"That's my Petrie-Dish." I tilted my head toward my security officer. "And my Lissa. Always looking out for me."

The former smirked while the latter frowned.

I didn't care so long as they were both beside me.

"CAREFUL NOW," Petrie said.

I waved her away. "Doc, I'm fine. All patched up. Walking and talking even." I allowed my legs to wobble, and many arms reached out to catch me.

When I laughed, Lissa lobbed a punch at my shoulder. "That's not funny, Captain."

I chuckled harder as they escorted me to the common area. Everyone stopped outside the door, and Lissa waved her hand. "Captain's first."

The door slid open, and when I stepped into the room, my eyes watered at the assault of lights. Greens and reds and whites twinkled, and a potted ivy sat in the corner. Someone, or perhaps several someones, had perched a flameless candle in the pot. Some damned fool had painted the thing a merry set of red and green stripes. The socks hanging across the wall were full of lumps and bumps, and a small box sat at the ivy's base.

"What's all this now?" I asked, and Seb grinned.

"Christmas!"

There was a hole in the wall where the shortest sock had been. Zac's. Lissa caught my frown and said, "We burned it, along with his body. While you were recovering, we blew up what remained of the *Lucky Fish*."

My strength left me, and I stumbled. Jake shoved a chair under me, and I fell into it. "But--"

"Don't worry, we stripped her bare first. We got the black box data, too," she said and patted my arm. "It was a good haul all things considered. We should be able to get some fresh food at the next fueling station."

Seb picked up the small box and handed it to me. "Happy Christmas!"

Someone, probably Seb by the way he grinned, had bundled the box with a shirt and tied a silly knot at the top. My fingers fumbled with the thin rope until Lissa took pity on me and cut the fool thing.

"It is not fresh food, but perhaps you will find it equally enjoyable," said Seb.

Inside the box was the snow globe.

The twinkling lights overhead reflected off the flakes inside making them dance. I stared at it while my vision did a little dance of its own.

"Damn dust on this ship. Time to cycle the air again," I said as I wiped my eyes with the back of my hand.

Lissa handed me a tissue. "We found it in...in Zac's quarters. We figured you'd want it, seeing how it was your father's."

"Thanks. What'd you find on the black box?"

The crew, who'd been digging through their "stockings" full of vitamin-candy, ceased moving at my question. Lissa took a deep breath and answered. "Junto admitted to paying Zac 500,000 credits to kill your father, though Junto wasn't the only one looking for him. He was wanted by the Family of Europa as well as crime syndicates in three other systems. Looks like this Santa thing was one of his covers. When Junto put out his request, Zac promised the Family he'd take care of him in exchange for the cash and a ship of his own."

"How'd you pull that info out of Junto?"

Lissa glanced at Petrie. "I made a deal."

I tried to stand and failed.

"I never said I wouldn't alert the authorities," she said and I laughed. "The black box contained brief notes from the captain of the *Lucky Fish*. It seems he bought Nick's cover story and tried to protect him from Junto's boys. The captain hid him in that closet. Some protective shelter, I guess. It had its own oxygen system, which is how Nick survived post-battle. Gave him a shot of adrenaline to keep him going in the cold when the heat went out on the *Lucky Fish*. Junto's boys couldn't find him because their ship was too damaged in the fight."

I asked, "How'd Zac know about the request?"

"He's been on Junto's radar for a while. Managed to snake a long list of jobs out of Junto that were shunted our way so Zac could perform side-jobs for the Family. When we arrived at the *Lucky Fish*, he found a single life source on board. The one Junto said might be there. We had the new scanners, so we picked up what 'the boys' had not. Zac hacked the *Lucky Fish*'s computer and flooded the safe room with carbon monoxide."

Seb curled his hands into fists around his empty sock. "And while we were chasing salvage, he set the controller back to confuse the investigation. He may have succeeded had I not found the body."

"Junto knew we were in the sector, so it was the perfect opportunity to do what his boys had failed to do," said Lissa.

I swallowed the lump in my throat. "All this because he wanted to be First Officer. Felt like I'd slighted him."

"Is that what he told you?" Lissa asked.

I nodded.

"How did you deduce he was the murderer?" asked Seb.

"Little things weren't adding up. The scanner that suddenly didn't work when it did, the logs that were too perfect, the salvage job when we needed it most. The helmets crackling and such. We'd just replaced them-- seemed weird to have them malfunctioning only when we needed to communicate most. I'm embarrassed to say this, but the black box of the *Lucky Fish* should have been a red flag. Even in a damaged ship, we should've been able to pull something from it, yet we got no response. Zac had cut all reserve power to it. I had to hit the manual reset button to restore it after reconnecting it. All the info from Junto helped point me in the right direction. Suppose I owe him for that."

I flicked a peppermint across the table where it glanced off Petrie's arm. She stared at the cellophane wrapper a moment too long before she met my gaze. "He reproduced the methods and tried to kill us all in our rooms. Only two people on the ship could do that--the captain and--"

"--Someone able to hack the computer. Our killer," I said. Little piles of candy were strewn across the table, but we sat silently while the red and green lights made pretty patterns on the wall.

I stood up in a rush and clapped my hands together. "Look, Zac was bitter and angry about change. I don't know about you, but I can't spend my time looking over my shoulder for the what if 's and why's. No more jealousy and stalking people and the like. If you've gotta beef, say it. If you can't say it to me, say it to someone. We're supposed to be a family here."

My gaze crossed Seb's and he gave a brief nod of his head. He'd need watching still, especially if he was reporting back to Junto...

Jake grinned and held up a small flask. "I agree, Captain. I say we celebrate the holiday with a quart of my uncle's finest."

"Finest what?" Petrie asked as she sniffed the proffered container. "Is that intended to be drinkable?"

Jake set glasses on the table, and my medic poured a splash or two into each one.

"I propose a toast," said Seb, and he held up his glass. "That is what you do on Earth, is it not?"

The crew laughed as five glasses glittered, though from the overhead lights or the uncle's alcohol, I couldn't say.

"A toast then," said Lissa. Several glasses clanked too early, and Jake held his side with one hand as he laughed. Desperation might have driven us to it, but under the programmed Christmas lights, we were alive and grateful. "To our captain, who brought us all together."

"And to Father Christmas!" Seb shouted.

"To Father Christmas," they echoed.

"Here's to you, Dad," I whispered.

The booze burned like three suns going down, and Lissa hooted. "Happy Christmas indeed! You got any more of that stuff, Jake?"

"I do! My Christmas present to each of you, I guess."

"Did I ever tell you about how I met our great captain?" Lissa said.

I groaned. There wasn't enough hooch in the galaxy to keep my ears from burning through this story, but I grinned anyway and took another drink.

I was with the only family that mattered, and it was a happy Christmas indeed.

ABOUT *OL' St. Nick*

Originally published in *Joy to the Worlds: Mysterious Speculative Fiction for the Holidays* (Grey Sun Press) and later reprinted as a standalone novella, *Ol' St. Nick* came from listening to the radio in December. Many of the Christmas carols about Santa Claus feel quite creepy when you think too long about the lyrics, including *Jolly Ol' St. Nicholas*. I knew I wanted to write a closed-in mystery in space. I just needed a main character...and a mobster Santa.

THE CEILING'S right corner is made up of 375—no, 376—knock-down plaster dots. A popcorn ceiling gone right, I guess. Despite the fact that it's 12:36 A.M. and I'm wakefully staring at the cream ceiling, I lose count somewhere in the left corner.

I shut my eyes in yet another attempt at sleep, but my mind refuses to stop spinning.

Spinning, spinning, spinning. Words. Pictures. Another scenario jammed through my brain at break-neck speeds until I want to scream.

Why in the hell do I need to remember the quadratic equation at 12:39 A.M.?

But then, math is better than thinking about the day—a day filled with flames shooting high into the air as a chorus of pops and hisses surround city after city, town after town. I close my eyes for a moment and her picture appears.

I don't know her. I just saw her picture online today. A flash of pride as she held her toddler close. Her husband's arm draped across her shoulders as they smiled for the camera. While strangers, the family from the online article had dreamed of happier moments, of a future when their family increased by one. A time not now, with the world raining fire and ash and death.

My eyes snap open as I count flattened dots, but they don't save me from the monster.

A couple and their child burned fleeing the Portland fires today, raising the death count to—

I need to shift my focus to something else. Something to hide me from the reality outside.

First, I try slow breathing, but every inhale fills my lungs with the remains of someone's life.

Of *someone*.

Wood, books, and photos. Skin and bone.

The death count rises to 78 today as the wildfires spread—

All I want is sleep. As if the silence of it will bring peace. My journey with the Sandman plagues me with horrors these days. If it's not the actual virus chasing us all down empty corridors, then it's rampant flames devouring half the country.

This time when I take a deep breath, I cough—a crackling sound that rips from my throat and reminds me of what bloodshot skies bring.

Pretty to look at, even prettier to share on social media, but hellish on the body.

Help withheld from states ravaged by fires as the federal government claims states should be able to help them—

Someone online once told me about a trick, and I try it now, painting a picture of a claw-footed bathtub in my mind. In reality, my hands are tucked at my sides. Eyes closed, they grip the tub's cold porcelain as water rushes out of the faucet.

Warm water. Clean water.

Water not burning from soot and ash and hell.

Firefighters struggle to gain control of South Seattle fires as thousands flee—

Into the tub it goes.

12:58 A.M. and my wrinkled fingers toss the firefighters into the water. Thousands of Seattlelites join them as they swirl down my visualized drain.

All too soon the water's gone, and my arms hang over the tub's porcelain sides. But the life raft doesn't hold back the thought.

What if the flames come here?

My mind sketches a map with a neon arrow pointing out the last fire's location.

Twenty miles feels forever away when walking, but fires furl and fold to their own rhythm. If I have five minutes to flee, what do I grab?

As I make a mental list, something furry stretches across my bare foot. No covers tonight. Too hot. Too stifling in the smoke. It buzzes in the back of my brain, and I sketch the tub hastily, willing it filled with water a second too late as the question stampedes across my mind.

What if I have to leave the cats behind?

My eyes fly open as I breathe haggardly in the darkness. The cats are here. I'm here. We're safe.

For now.

I try and toss imaginary dead cats down my mental drain, but even their fake destruction is too much for me. Statistics isn't a topic I enjoy, yet I can't help but calculate how many pets were left behind as people fled the West Coast this week.

The tub's faucet is dripping, and I count each precious drop of water, desperate for a release from the monster within my mind—the anxiety that paints images worse than any streaming video. I refuse to turn and face the hypercolor flames on my right for fear they might be real.

Instead, I whisper the word along with the action. Drip...drip...drip.

Police arrested a man along I-5, spotted setting a fire in the median—

Drip. Nothing else. Drip...drip...

Deer flee, and I push my way past them to focus on the tub in front of me.

Drip!

If I can just sleep, then I'll wake up tomorrow. One day closer to the rains that promise to crush the fires raging across forests and cities alike, yet all I can think about—*No.*

Drip! Drip!

What if the fires come while I'm asleep? Will I hear the alarms over the—

DRIP!

—Over this damn dripping? What's leaking anyway?

DRIP!

Something tickles my nose. It's probably a stray hair moved by the ceiling fan.

Could it be ash?
DRIP!
Maybe it's rain!
The thud that splashes against my window isn't metaphorical. It doesn't land in a tub but rolls down the glass until it lands on the ground.
Drip!
Drip?
This time, my eyes stay closed. My breath doesn't slow much, not with the congestion in my lungs, but it slows just enough as it moves to the rhythm outside...
Drip.

ABOUT "DRIP"

Originally published in *99 Tiny Terrors* (Pulse Publishing), this is one of the shortest stories I've written and one of my favorites. I often have insomnia and with it, counting sheep does nothing for me. I've tried everything and honestly, the bathtub trick in the story didn't work either, but it did spin up an interesting story idea.

LEVEL UP

MICKEY'S WAS A GOOD ONE. You could always count on their dumpsters to have something edible in them, or at least, that's what I'd been told this morning by a woman pushing a shopping cart. I spotted a cold English muffin and grabbed it with gloved hands. Had to scrape the dirt off the corner, but I figured the dirt couldn't hurt me any more than being outside in the winter.

I was about to bite into it when I smelled something worse than a dirty dumpster. Shit mixed with booze and the hint of something...sweet?

When I turned around, a homeless man stood five feet away. The way he smiled sent goosebumps across my bare arms that had nothing to do with the cold.

"I got here first," I said.

He stepped closer, and I gagged. The English muffin no longer sounded like a good idea, and I shoved it into the pocket of my flannel.

"New to the life, eh, love?"

Keeping one eye on him, I shoved some trash aside as I dug one-handed through the dumpster.

"These big places with their fancy food printers won't have much of nothing. You got lucky with that muffin, see? They recycle the food waste. But I can show ya where to score some good 'ol fish and chips iffen ye don't mind them being a bit soggy."

Maybe my nose had adjusted since my stomach grumbled at the thought. When was the last time I'd had fish? Had it been before or after the divorce? I shook my head. "Anyone who's offering to share is trouble. Stay away from me."

He shrugged. "Look, it ain't always safe out here for folks like yerself."

"Folks like me?" I asked.

"Ya know, trans? If anything, ya need a guide. Someone to show you the ropes and where it's safe and whatnot."

I pulled my hair closer about my face. How could he tell? I'd been passing a long time now, though I supposed without my meds things could've changed. "What's in it for you? Why help me?" With nothing else to eat from the dumpster, I let the lid slam shut.

"I'm just payin' it forward. Like someone did for me. You'll do the same for someone else sometime in the future. We all do...at least those of us who ain't trouble. Besides, you don't wanna get caught..."

Just the suggestion of the sweeps made my legs tremble, and he nodded.

"Good. So you already know 'bout them sweeps. Got to avoid them. And the weeps."

I tilted my head. "The weeps?"

"The sadness. It'll come on ya when you wake up and realize yer in hell. I'm Ben. You don't gotta tell me yer name. Not everyone does or even remembers. I've been Ben for about five years now."

He held out a dirty hand, and his roughened skin prickled me through my gloves.

"I'm...Sara."

"Nice to meet you, Sara." With a head tilt, he gestured for me to follow along. We passed a few more fast food places, a community store, and a gas station before reaching Fourth Avenue.

"Wait, we can't cross Fourth," I said as I stopped at the intersection. The side I stood on was run down, buildings in need of repair and love. Across the way, I could see skyscrapers in the distance. Wealth began at Fourth and increased exponentially the closer one got to downtown.

His crooked finger pointed at the corner. "We're not goin' far, just there a ways. Sometimes ya gotta take risks iffen ya want to eat."

Despite the dread in the pit of my stomach, I followed him across the street and into an alleyway. A mix of sea brine and sour met my nose long before we reached our destination.

Unlike Mickey's dumpster, this one bore a fresh coat of paint and sat in one of the cleanest alleys I'd ever seen. I didn't have to watch where I stepped to avoid trash or needles or dead animals. The place looked downright clean, if not recently scrubbed, and visions of the sweeps ran through me.

"Are you sure this is safe?" I asked as I gestured. "This place is clean, like it's been swept clean."

Ben tossed open the garbage bin's lid. Rot nearly bowled me over as I gagged.

"Looks like today's a good day," he said, and I stepped back.

Rotten fish could make one sicker than dirt, and I wanted no part in it.

He reached in and grabbed a plastic bag full of partly frozen fish. "See here? They mix the good stuff in with the rotten, but ya can tell by the bag ties. Red means it's a goner, but green means they couldn't sell it. Might be 'cause no one wanted it or maybe the fish ain't look perfect or somethin'. Either way, perfectly eatable."

I followed him from the alleyway at a distance and sighed when we crossed Fourth Avenue and back into poor side of town. Two blocks over, he led me into a lean-to of plywood and sheets of metal, most of it rusted and sharp. Careful not to cut myself, I wiggled through the opening and found myself in a much larger space than had been visible from outside.

The abandoned building held a couple dozen folks, all of them homeless and all of them wary. A few nodded in Ben's direction but otherwise remained next to their own small encampments.

Ben's place consisted of an old tent and a metal barrel. He tossed a few sticks from a pile inside of it and used a lighter from his pocket to light it. In the distance, those who'd nodded to him approached and formed a short line nearby.

He unwrapped the bag and jabbed a fish with a stick before handing it to the first person. The fish didn't last long as he passed them out, including me in the process, and we stood in silence, roasting our fish on his flaming barrel.

At least these smelled right.

"So, I take it yer hiding from the law?" asked Ben, and I jumped. "It's cool. These folks ain't gonna rat on ya. We take care of our own down here in the Village."

The man beside me unbuttoned his shirts to expose his chest where a bright red "T" glared angrily against his skin. "I was caught when the laws first came down and the raids started. Ran as fast as I could. No family was going to risk protecting me."

Lighter scars from arm pit to arm pit noted a previous surgery, and he nodded when I spotted it. Like me, he'd found himself fleeing a world that wished us dead.

"My husband turned me in," I whispered, and those huddled around the fire murmured in response. "After the divorce, he didn't have any reason not to, so I came home the next day to find I didn't have a home. I didn't have a car, no bank account, no ch-children. Nothing."

Ben patted my shoulder. "This is why ya need a guide. Folks to protect ya. We take care of our own here."

I bit into the crunchy fish. Juice dripped down my chin, and I wiped it with my hands before licking them clean. "The Village, eh? How do you avoid the sweeps?"

"Most of the time, they don't cross Fourth, but iffen they do, we have lookouts. We can hear 'em and we hide. Got lots of places to hide iffen ya know where to look..."

"Them sweeps are bad news. They do things to ya there. Bad things. You ain't the same no more," said the man with the T on his chest.

"What, like conversion therapy or something?" I asked.

"Worse."

Ben patted my shoulder. "Don't ya worry 'bout it. We ain't gonna get caught in no sweep. Stick with us and you'll be okay."

He slid another piece of fish in my direction, and I accepted it gratefully.

I STOOD in front of Fourth Avenue, blood dripping from my dirty coat. In front of me lay one of the men from the Village, the one who'd been looking at me sideways for a good few months, and I dropped the switchblade Ben had given me for protection. I hadn't meant to kill him, but when he'd grabbed for my pants, my body took over. One moment he'd come at me, and the next, he lay on the ground bleeding out from where I'd stabbed him multiple times.

My brain told me to run, to flee, but where would I go?

The Village takes care of its own.

Somehow I didn't think it mattered that the guy had attacked me. Ben couldn't defend me against everyone there, and as he'd said, they took care of their own. I'd be dead before tomorrow if I went back. But standing in front of First, I was as good as dead too, so I turned away and ran, panic taking me down streets at random.

A few miles from the Village I stopped, my breath haggard. I'd never killed someone before. My hands shook as I leaned against the brick wall. I was still leaning there when a siren chirped nearby, and I shot off in the opposite direction. Whether it was the cops or a sweep didn't matter. Either meant danger. Either meant death.

I turned a corner and slammed into a guy wearing a dark suit who smelled of aftershave. The same kind my ex had worn.

He grabbed my wrists and frowned. "Hey, hey, it's okay. Are you hurt?"

"Lemme go!"

"Look, you've got blood on you. Are you hurt? Do you need help?"

His voice was deep like Ben's. The familiarity mixed with lost adrenaline left me slumped before him. I didn't have it in me to keep running, and he wrapped his arm around my shoulder.

"Is this your blood, honey? Or does it belong to the man who came at you?"

I tumbled backward, but someone else stood behind me, someone who blocked my escape from the alleyway. Fear ripped at my voice, and I couldn't scream, not that anyone would've done a thing to help. I'd tumbled from one danger into another.

"I'm Caleb," the man said as he approached and pressed something metallic against my neck. A prick, then cold as something shot into me, and my muscles went limp. "There now, isn't that much better?"

A sweep. That's what this was. My teeth chattered as I stared at him.

He picked me up with ease and carried me to a vehicle, where I was tucked into the back seat. The buildings grew taller, then shorter again as we passed through downtown and off to the other side of the city. It was a neighborhood I hadn't seen since before the divorce and then only once when we'd visited my ex's boss for dinner. Stylish cars and designer pets were the minimum for membership into this 'hood. The car pulled to a stop beside a fancy restaurant with an Italian name, and I blinked at it as I tried to focus.

"You're going to love it at *Ristorante di Massimiliano*. Best Italian this side of the pond," said Caleb as he helped me out of the vehicle.

I stumbled twice on the few steps leading to the door, but once inside, the place assaulted me with smells of fresh bread, tomatoes, and herbs. My mouth watered as he led me to a back room and gently set me onto a chair. I'd no more than sat before a waiter entered carrying plates of food, which he placed before me like I was a queen.

"Vino, Signore?" the waiter asked, and Caleb shook his head.

"No, acqua per favore." Of me he asked, "I assume water is okay with you?"

I stared at the plates of food as my stomach growled.

"Nod yes."

The moment he said it, my brain complied.

"Have something to eat. I know you must be hungry after a year or two on the streets."

Again my brain followed his instructions, and I bit my tongue. How was he doing that? I'd had no intention of following his directions, but there I was, doing everything he said.

As if he'd read my mind, he smiled. "The shot I gave you does more than make you relax. It makes you pliable, suggestable if you will."

My throat was tight, but after a swallow of water, it loosened enough for me to clear it. "Why? Why not just kill me?"

His laughter echoed in the mostly empty room. "Kill you? Why would I do that? Oh no, you're much too valuable a commodity now. What do you think of the food?"

The fork stopped halfway to my mouth. When had I started eating? I had every intention of setting it down, but I bit into the chicken parmesan. I thought I might die at the taste alone, and across the table, Caleb laughed.

"Does it bother you that you're eating while wearing bloody clothes?" he asked.

"Not really. I've worn worse. This is real food, isn't it? Not the rep shit?"

He moved so fast, across the table like a leopard, and he slapped me hard across the face. "Here I am feeding you a good meal and you sully it with a word like that?"

I winced but the drugs inside me continued to shovel food into my mouth.

"And no, this isn't replicated food. It's the real deal. Have you ever seen a replication plant?"

When I shook my head, he smiled.

"You're going to see one today for today is just the beginning for you. A chance at a new, real life..."

❦

FROM WHERE I stood in the shadows, the young man had his back to me as he rooted around in the garbage can. Not thin enough to have been on the streets for very long, but a touch underweight meaning he was newer. He didn't hear me until I touched his shoulder, and he spun around, knife in hand.

"Whatdya want? This is mine."

I nodded. "Of course it is. You look new. Haven't seen you around before. You got a guide yet?"

He closed the garbage can with one hand while his fingers gripped his knife like a lifeline. "Go away."

"Hey, I'm not here to hurt you. It's just everyone needs a guide at first." The expression on his face was one I knew well. I'd worn it too when I'd first met Ben, and he'd offered me a safe haven. The young man frowned at me, and I held up my hands. "I'll leave you alone if that's what you want."

"Wait—" he said as I began to turn away. "What's in it for you?"

"I'm just payin' it forward. Like someone did for me. I can show you where to score better food and the like."

His eyes wandered to the skyscrapers above him.

Poor kid was far past Fourth Avenue, and he was so far out of his league it hurt.

"Them rich folks with homes are willing to pay a pretty penny for food that ain't been replicated. So much that they'll eat anything," he said as he stepped toward me. "You ever seen a rep plant?"

I had, but I wasn't about to tell him that. He was speaking the lines I was about to and when I stared at him, I saw the shift in his demeanor. Gone was the young man, freshly homeless. Instead, a predator stood before me, and I stuck my hands in my pockets, at ease. I shook my head and allowed my eyes to go wide. "I haven't."

"Ever wonder where all that comes from?"

"What?"

"The stuff. The material for printing food."

Another step closer, and he was in reach. I fiddled with the blade in my pocket as I glanced at his feet.

"Sorry, love, but everyone has to eat," he said.

"They do." I smile and when he came at me, I stepped sideways. Before he could run at me again, I stabbed him in the chest. "Been watching you going on two days now. Never knew you were one of us. Too bad."

Blood spurted across his lips as he tried to breathe.

"I ain't your love, but as you said, folks gotta eat." I let his body drop to the pavement below and waited.

Caleb approached a few minutes later with a wide grin. "That's number four for you, #618. One more and it's promotion time."

I eyed his clean clothes with disdain. "Sure, a promotion." I held out my hand as my mouth watered. The juicy burger in his pocket hit my nose and for a moment, I considered making him my fifth kill.

"Uh, uh. That won't get you a promotion."

"What?" I asked.

"Taking me out. You have to know your place. Maybe one day you'll get a home like me. A better spouse. Might be on the bottom floor and the husband might have buck teeth, but one day. Just keep doing your job." He handed her the burger.

I didn't scarf it right there in the alleyway, though I wanted to. Instead, I waited until I'd turned the corner and ducked in the rep plant nearby. The guards didn't stop me—the blood on me proof enough of who I was now—and I set out for the cafeteria, careful not to run and show how hungry I was.

I recognized most of the faces in the large room, though they were face down in their own burgers, their rotting teeth making a mess of the recycled patties.

When I sat down, I nodded to them first before unwrapping my own burger. Was it someone I'd known? Maybe someone I'd killed for the rep plant? The thought gave me pause for a moment, but only for a moment.

After all, everyone has to eat.

I bit into my burger and smiled.

ABOUT "LEVEL UP"

Someone once asked me what I thought homelessness would look like in the future. "Level Up" is, sadly, where my brain went. I hope that humanity will do better, that we'll help people find their way into having a home, food, clothes, and health care—human rights—but I suspect we won't. Greed rules us and honestly, I feel this story hits way too close to home. We'd do it if we could.

SCOUT'S HONOR

I NEVER WANTED to work with the cartel.

Mi abuela wanted better for her little Pia Fernandez. Before the Yellow Stone sent fire and ash into the sky, *su abuela,* her grandmother, studied weather, and *su madre* was a doctor. A long line of women with more to their name than a few scraps of food. But all of that changed with *mi padre.* He had connections and influence—at least before the ghost fleet murdered him. The day I inherited his airship, *La Hermana del Bendito Sol,* or *The Blessed Sun's Sister,* I inherited everything else, including his *mala suerte,* or bad luck. Now, only fools would be willing to crew *La Hermana.*

Knowing that, I ignored the usual haunts of those looking for work and set off for *el último muelle,* the last pier in Mexico City, where broken down fools waited on broken down docks for fools like me to hire them. Only thrill seekers and thieves, their desperation smelling as strongly as their sweat, would take a chance out there. Before I could open my mouth, a shadow rose before me, and the fools lining the old pier skittered down a nearby alleyway. Only two people could make us turn to dust—Jefe, or his second in command, Two Cross.

"*Oye, chica. ¿Qué pasa?*" Two-Cross's gravelly voice mixed with the creaking planks beneath his heavy boots as he stepped up beside me. Like most cartel *familias,* he wore a gold cross, but Two-Cross wore his in both jewelry and skin, as black ink marred his face with the ornate holy symbol.

"I need work," I said.

"There's no work for you here."

"*Mierda.*" I removed the plastic board from my backpack and set it in front of him. "You posted this job yesterday, and I know it ain't been filled 'cause it was still marked available when I removed it."

Two-Cross leaned close to me, his breath a mix of booze and decay. Much as my feet wished to tumble backward, I remained still, my nose almost touching his. "Lucky for you, Jefe has a task he wants done."

I let loose a string of profanities in *Pocho,* or Spanglish. There was work, and then there were Jefe's *tasks*. "And am I meant to survive this?"

Two-Cross shrugged. "You know Monterrey Tower?" he asked.

"You know I do. It's where *mi padre* was killed."

"Sí. *Tu papá* was there to get tech for Jefe. He failed. Now *you* get tech for Jefe."

I nodded, my tongue thick in my mouth. "What will I get if I do this?"

"You get to live. *Maybe* you get your honor back."

"I'll need a crew."

He raised his hand—the one missing an index finger—and waggled it in the air. Two men and a woman slinked out of the shadows as they eyed me with suspicion. All human—or as human as any of us were these days.

"These three owe Jefe. They'll be your crew."

"Three ain't enough to crew *La Hermana,* and you know it."

When he wigged his fingers in the air a second time, another dozen or more shadows became solid as they stepped into the sun. "They all owe Jefe, so they'll listen to you if they know what's good for them."

With no other choice, I nodded. Jefe says *saltar*, you jump. I set off down the pier with lean fools trailing behind me. My skin crawled from Two-Cross's gaze on my back as I stepped over places where planks had long since dropped away from the pier. He was probably wishing I'd fall through and save everyone the trouble.

La Hermana del Bendito Sol lay at the pier's end—there was nowhere else I was allowed to stow her—but from her spot in the city,

Teotihuacan stretched out across the land beneath us like a promise that there were still things of beauty in this world.

I set my jaw firmly as we steered away from our floating city and towards my future, whatever it would be.

THE HALF-FINISHED, half-flooded Monterrey City lay to the north, and to the east lay what little remained of old tropical forests and their pyramids. We flew over the Avenue of the Dead as we approached *Teotihuacan*, the Pyramid of the Moon, while to the west of us rose a lengthy mountain range with its own unpredictable weather system. Somewhere along our path traveled the powerful ghost fleet, with airships that could hide amidst both cloud and sun, and attack before a captain had done little more than gasp. Or so it was rumored.

Mi padre's death brought few details as no crew members survived. One moment, he'd reached Monterrey and the next, he had been gone. When he didn't return, I bartered the last of my savings to the cartel, which had found his battered ship downed in a valley. No other ships could make burn marks like the ghost fleet, so when Jefe reported to *mi abuela* that her son and his crew were lost to the ghosts, rumor became solid. Became fact.

An inexperienced captain would take the forest route, but the ghosts would expect that. Something I kept in mind as I ordered my crew to the west.

"Captain." Juan pointed in the distance where the gray haze of rain lay. Like the rest of him, his arm sported enough ink to be more black than brown. "We goin' through that?"

"We are."

"It's monsoon season."

Pamella, a woman who resembled *mi abuela* in both stature and attitude, frowned. "That a problem?"

"You'd no more fly a plane than an airship through that kinda wind. As much as we got engines and rudders, this thing still follows air currents." When I furrowed my brow, Juan added, "Been running crew for Jefe long time. I know how a ship works."

Pamella's eyes grew wide as she turned to face me.

"No offense, but flying through that sounds like a bad plan, and we're here to make sure Jefe gets what's his."

"It's either that or face the ghosts," I said as I pointed at my map. "You knew the risks when you walked on board. Make sure we've got enough lift. Wouldn't help us to snag ourselves on *Cerro's* peak."

Around us, grand waterfalls dumped torrents of water down the rocky mountainside, and in the distance, the familiar saddle-shape of *Cerro de la Silla* appeared through the haze. As the clouds darkened, rain splashed against the bridge's windows.

"Hey, Captain," said Pamella. "Something on the screen."

I scooted over to where she manned the reverse periscope, and she pointed to airship remains a dozen meters ahead. If I hadn't been sailing *La Hermana del Bendito Sol*, I could almost swear I was staring at my ship's remains, right down to the scorch marks on her bow.

"Let's check it out."

"You thinking there might be something worth salvaging?" asked Pamella.

"Maybe. Could be the weather took them down. Could be the ghosts. Either way, they weren't expecting to land in that basin. Take us lower, Juan."

A retort shone in his eyes, but the words rested on his thin lips and remained there as our approach revealed the shadow of someone or something moving near the ship itself.

"What is it? Could it be a bear?" asked Juan.

"Doubtful. Could be a survivor. Maybe someone willing to pay for their safe return to Mexico City." I watched through the periscope as we drew closer to the ground. My bino-glasses zoomed in, giving me a grainy image. There was no mistaking the lengthy shadow that moved among the debris. Too tall for a human. Too tall for anything but a scout.

Our ship light reflected off purple-gold eyes, painting an eerie mask on a rather gaunt being. Rather than hide, they stood tall as the rain poured down from the sky. "Stay behind me," I said as I slid my arms through my raincoat's sleeves. "It's a scout, and they're fairly jumpy. If there's something worth salvaging, they could be the key to finding it."

"Is it true that scouts have magic?" asked Juan.

I shook off the greedy look in his eyes and scowled. "It ain't magic. Just something different is all."

The wind buffeted my small airship and me, once I opened the doors. In the downpour, I couldn't see but a half meter in front of me, and I tapped the focusing dial on my glasses, and the lens zoomed in on the scout and the wreckage behind him. Plastic and metal framing mixed with the balloon's torn fabric, while random personal effects lay scattered in charred piles.

"Maybe he can tell us what happened."

I spun on my heel to glare at Juan, a look he couldn't see with my bino-glasses in the way.

He held up his hands. "I didn't mean nothing by it. Not magic, just what happened to the ship. If he was here when it went down."

My insides quaked more than I liked, and I took a deep breath to steady myself. Jefe's fools, dangerous though they might be, needed me to find *mi padre's* tech. Rather than expecting a knife in the back, I returned to the scene before us, a forced smile plastered across my face.

"Hello? *¡Hola!*"

There was nowhere to take shelter in those remains, so I gestured for the scout to approach my ship. At first, his eyes grew shadowed as he glanced over my head, but when the wind buffeted us all with a wave of water, he darted forward with much longer and faster strides than I could make.

Mi padre's scout had been reclusive. Too busy to interact with a kid like me. This one didn't seem to be the same, which gave me pause. The four of us settled in my ship's tiny dining space, where we gathered around a lone table. I wiped a clump of hair from where it had plastered against my face, then smiled at our visitor.

"I'm Captain Pia of *La Hermana del Bendito Sol*. We were heading toward Monterrey when the crew spotted ship remains. From the debris pattern, it appears to have smashed against the rocks, after getting hit by...something. Was this your ship?" I glanced up at him, craning my neck up to his great height, and gestured for him to have a seat.

The gold in his eyes softened until only purple remained. "I am Diego Aparicio of Veracruz, though some to the north call me Doug.

Captain Hendricks out of Texas piloted the ship, *The Strong Birds*. The weather spoke of a creeping cloud that spread across the mountains between thunderclaps, but Captain Hendricks would not hear of it. 'The weather does not speak,' he said to me before the ghosts arrived."

Rather than folding himself awkwardly into a seat, he perched on the chair's back. The membranes between his arms and ribs folded in on themselves, leaving long gaps at his leather vest's sides. While he talked, I poured hot water into mugs and splashed dried tea leaves into my own. His smooth face spoke of youth, but with so little known about his kind, I wasn't ready to assume it. "What do you know of this area?" I asked.

"Not much. Honestly, I have not been to Mexico in a long while."

Making it unlikely he'd heard of *mi familia*. That could work to my benefit. "Were there no survivors in the crash?" I asked, and he shook his head.

"So, how'd you live? Do you have ma—"

I kicked Juan beneath the table.

"The captain, he was mad. Something about the storm confused him. When I told him the storm would see us crashed along the mountainside, he refused to listen. I had no choice but to leave."

"You mean you abandoned your ship," I said.

The scout nodded as he settled his hands around the warm tea mug.

"You said you chose to serve with *The Strong Birds*, but where were you before that?" I asked.

"With my tribe. *The Strong Birds* was my first ship."

I nodded confirmation, but Juan stood and tossed his cup toward the waste bin. "Captain, he ain't nothing but a *pendejo*, a coward. We should leave him here to rot with the rest of his crew. He'll only bring trouble."

Purple met my brown as Diego looked at me expectantly.

"Anything worth salvaging from the remains?" I asked.

"Beyond damaged framing? No, nothing survived the fall down the mountain. Less survived the ghosts," he said and closed his eyes. "Scavengers cleaned the bodies down to the bone, then dragged those off soon after, and the balloon cloth was too shredded even to use as a shield from the storms."

My glass's lens sharpened when I glanced at his gaunt frame, made gaunter by the way his ribs protruded at weird angles from his torso. "When's the last time you ate?"

He shrugged but took another sip of warm tea.

"Look, you ain't a coward. I know from *mi padre* that scouts carry more than weather-sense with them, they carry honor. No one messes with a scout or their crewmembers, so if you're willing to help get us to Monterrey, I'll feed you and make sure you get back to Mexico City. From there, well, where you go is entirely up to you."

"You're heading to Monterrey?" he asked, and it was my turn to nod. "The dead lay between here and there, sheltered in invisible metal that rains fire across the sky."

"The ghost fleet," I whispered, and beside me, Pamella shuddered. "Will we make it to Monterrey? Can we?"

"I do not see the future, Captain Fernandez."

Heat spread across my cheeks. "My apologies, Scout Diego. The storm's severe. I only meant to inquire after its progress through the mountain range. And please, Captain Pia if you will."

He glanced off to his left as if my ship's walls were see-through, then cleared his throat. "We should hurry."

I was moving before my mind caught up with my legs. "Pamella, get him something to eat. Everyone else, bridge," I called as I ran.

Perhaps the coward would cost me everything.

Or perhaps *mi padre's* spirit was with me after all. Perhaps he'd placed the scout in my path so I could find my way home again.

RAIN BATTERED my ship as we approached Monterrey, though the water more closely resembled fists than tiny droplets. With each mile passed, I held my breath tighter as Diego and I scanned the skies for the ghost fleet. Thunder rumbled in the distance, then approached like one of Jefe's moods—all sound and fury.

If the ghost fleet was out there, they hid themselves well, and I turned to Diego. "Can...can you see the ghost fleet? When they're hidden?"

He gave the briefest of nods, and behind us, Juan gasped.

"Juan, pay attention to steering the ship," I shouted over another bark of thunder. Up ahead, a clump of gray hovered and as we approached, my lenses focused enough to display the city of Monterrey. Its base, a mess of metal construction debris and overgrown moss, was a fifth the size of Mexico City. A handful of buildings reached up like fingers, their incomplete tops a gnarled mess of rebar and concrete. It didn't float so much as rest again the ground, its lowest layer crumbled into the mountainside.

"Take us to the right," I said as I pointed. A long wooden pier stuck out, complete with a metal anchor point. "You can anchor it but keep an eye out. That anchor's stuck in nothing but rot."

"Is it safe to dock there?" Juan gestured as the pier swayed with the gusting wind.

"If we land near the base, we'll have to climb over that mess. I don't know about you, but I don't wanna try that in this downpour. We'd slip and impale ourselves on rebar before we'd made it twenty feet."

As the ship brushed against the dock, wood creaked, and I winced as I locked the airship's controls. While the others stared at the developing lightning show outside, I slid the key into a hidden pocket in my shirt seam.

"Juan, go tether us, please. Preferably somewhere secure."

He cocked an eyebrow but set off to follow my command. I turned to the rest of my makeshift crew and forced my shoulders to relax.

"Scout Diego comes with me. You all will remain here and keep watch." I handed a short-range radio to Pamella. "If you see anything, call me on Channel 1."

"You trust us to stay with the ship?" asked Pamella, and I smiled.

"Jefe wants his tech. Without me, good luck finding it. Besides, you'd still have to escape the ghost fleet. I *might* be able to talk them out of killing us painfully. But you all? Let's just say they like their victims rough around the edges."

Her lips pursed together as she stared at Diego. "Separating a scout from their ship is bad luck, but it's on your head, Captain."

"What isn't?" I muttered.

Hard rain pelted us as Diego and I stepped outside. Juan had tied us to a metal hook bolted into a long pillar, and I leaned over to check his knots. "Good enough?" he shouted over the weather.

"They'll hold better than the pier will!" Ship secure, I gestured for Diego to follow me toward the city.

A low moan escaped the pier as another gust of wind rocked it, and he flinched.

"My redemption is necessary, Captain—maybe yours is too, considering this fool's errand—but this storm is nothing to trifle with." He pointed to the tallest tower towards the city's center. "Why enter a building in danger of collapse at any moment? What do you wish to prove?"

As we trudged through the rain, debris littered the streets as the wind screamed through mostly hollow buildings.

"I can't go back empty-handed," I shouted over the storm. "Otherwise, it's not worth going back. The cartel isn't forgiving."

"No, they are not."

The way he said it rang of pain and truth, and I asked, "So, what would a scout know of the cartel? No offense, but you ride around on airships, reading weather, right? There are so many rumors surrounding you scouts, it's hard to know what's truth, but people revere you. You're sought after like a prized piece of tech, while people like me, well, we're lucky if we live long enough to die, let alone have a *familia*."

The scout blinked at me, his eyes rapidly cycling between their purple and golden hues. "You are not the only one to know loss and pain. What use is there in flying if it is in service to a—never mind. There are many types of shackles, Captain Pia."

A chunk of concrete building lay across the cracked road we followed. While I crawled through a hollowed-out square at its corner, Diego leapt over the pillar with ease.

"Once with *mi padre*, his Scout leapt off the ship and rode the air currents down below us. There ain't any shackles on you that I can see. You could fly away right now, and I'd never find you. Me? My chains are forged by Jefe and the cartel. There's nowhere I can run that he wouldn't find me."

"Do not presume to know everything about Scouts and their lives,

Captain. To you, we are a commodity to use. There's a reason my people avoid Mexico City in favor of the Arizonas to the north."

The walk forward remained silent except for a few grunts as we hiked toward our goal. Thunder rattled the buildings a few times, sending small cascades of stone down the building's sides. Our eyes remained skyward as we waited for something larger to loom overhead, yet nothing more than storm clouds darkened our path.

Had it been finished, the building that stood before us could've been beautiful; stretching high above the other buildings by double, its stone columns were carved with intricate line work. It wasn't the line's maze-like formation that caught my eye, but the delicate tulip sketched beside the door.

"What is it?" asked Diego.

"*Mi padre* was here." I laid my hand against the mark, allowing its roughness to scratch my palm. "Jefe used to give him grief for having such a girlie mark, but *mi abuela* loves tulips. He said every time he drew one, it reminded him of her sacrifices."

I tugged on the door, which remained stuck, and after a good wrench, it flung open with the wind's assistance. If *mi padre* had left that mark, he had meant for me to find the tech.

"Is it safe to go inside? The building...she leans."

One corner of the building had sunk into the ground below, giving the building a noticeable tilt. I shook the door, and when the building remained standing, I shrugged. "She's solid enough."

Three feet inside, debris blocked our forward momentum. Muscles hid beneath Diego's slender frame, and I couldn't help but admire the efficiency in which he cleared a path for us toward a second set of doors.

These led to a windowless hallway that made my skin crawl. There was darkness and then there was this. I reached up to touch the side of my glasses, and a light beam shot forward, illuminating the area. Wider than I'd expected, the hall held three doors and a sitting area. Green moss covered what at one time must have been furniture but now had slickened into uselessness. Diego sneezed.

"Onward we go," I whispered as we passed through the first door.

A larger room, perhaps one that had served as storage, was empty of all but small rodents who fled my light for the various holes in the walls.

The faint smell of mold tickled my nose, but its source remained unknown. Another storage room met our exploration, but the third door led to another hall, with more doors leading us deeper into the building.

"If you are determined to find something, let us find it and be gone from this graveyard." Diego shuddered as he eyed the crumbling walls.

At first, several rooms we passed through were like the first, a mixture of mud and green moss, cracked from plants and animals that had reclaimed the areas as their own. Sometimes holes allowed a trickle of rain to find its way in, and soon we slogged our way through knee-deep water as we approached the sunken corner.

"There must be something important in this building. Why else would the ghost fleet be protecting it?" I asked.

"Who says they are protecting it?"

"Look, trust me. There's something here. If there was nothing here, then *mi padre* died for nothing. They killed him to keep him from it." I turned away to keep him from seeing my tears.

"If there is something of value here, where would it be?" he asked.

I pursed my lips. Where had *mi padre* looked when searching for goods? I glanced around the next room, but nothing popped out at me. No wall coverings at odd angles or lock boxes tucked beneath furniture. "Maybe we're on the wrong floor. I mean, the ground level isn't exactly where one hides important items."

"Or maybe there is nothing here. This city was never finished, so would your ancestors have kept anything of value here?"

He wasn't wrong, and I balled my hands into fists as we slogged through yet another waterlogged room. "There must be something. *Mi padre* didn't leave his mark for nothing," I whispered and then flinched as he heard me.

"Where does your cartel keep its valuables?" he asked.

"Most of the tech running the tower is at the city's inner core, in the lower levels. If the makers of this city were anything like the cartel, I assume they'd keep their goods in the basement like Jefe does." I shrugged. "It's not like they'd tell me. But unfinished? Maybe they kept their building libraries here."

"Building libraries?"

"Knowledge. On how they made the cities in the sky."

The scout pointed at a sign on the wall. Its stepped iconography indicated the stairs, and we followed them down two floors where the water reached my chest. "I don't think I can go down another level. This will have to do."

At a height of seven feet, water didn't bother Diego, and he pried open the door with ease. Metal shelving, bolted to the walls, stood stripped of anything useful. A few old, rusted wires draped from the ceiling, but otherwise, the room held more water than goods.

"Damn," I muttered.

"I have to ask, why bring me along, Captain? I could be—*should* be watching over the ship rather than searching for the unknown."

"I can't trust my crew, well, Jefe's crew. Backstabbing thieves, the lot of them. I certainly can't trust them to have my back."

"So, I am here to guard you and open doors?" When I nodded, he continued, "What makes you think your crew will not steal your ship?"

"Take *La Hermana del Bendito Sol*?" I laughed, and the sound echoed across the emptiness. The next room was stripped bare as well, as was the next, and I blinked back tears.

"Why is the thought of theft funny?"

"My ship's famous, Scout Diego. At least in Mexico. *Mi padre* captained her for twenty years, the whole time, running salvage for the cartel. Any man stupid enough to defy *mi padre's* wishes for me to fly her is a man looking for a cursed life."

One moment there was ground beneath me, and the next, the floor sank and I tumbled into cold, murky water with a gasp. My head broke the surface as I treaded water, while a current tugged at my clothing. My light flickered in and out, then failed, leaving me in sudden darkness. Panic rose from my belly, pushing out my air too fast, and I took too large a gasp. Water flooded my mouth as slender hands grabbed me by the shoulders and pulled diagonally until I stood on solid floor.

"Thank you," I said with a cough, then pointed back the way we'd come. "Perhaps we should go up a floor. Might be easier than drowning. Besides, anything under that much water is useless to us."

"It will take a while to return to the stairs. Especially in the dark like this."

I removed my glasses and blew on them in an attempt to dry their insides. After a moment or two, the light flickered on, weak but working. The pale beam illuminated a pile of plywood and metal bars in the corner, and I asked, "Could you break a hole in the ceiling with any of that? Maybe we could climb up as a shortcut."

The scout tilted his head as he examined the beams, then tested two metal bars. He thrust the heaviest into the ceiling tile several times as water poured forth, and wriggled the bar back and forth to expand the hole large enough to squeeze through. He lifted me through it easily before pulling himself into yet another room that had been stripped of tech.

Both of us sat on damp concrete to catch our breath, though I suspected we rested more for my benefit than his.

"How did you end up in possession of your father's ship?" he asked when we crossed into a room that had served as an office space.

I tugged open drawers and cabinet doors, searching for anything and finding nothing. A few scraps of paper and a dead mouse. "*Mi padre* was killed by the ghost fleet while...well, while searching this tower. He made it out, but they took down the ship. Cost me my entire savings to convince Jefe to search for him. Jefe's crew returned with the damaged ship. I...I owe him for her repairs."

The scout's eyes grew wide. "Your father was Thomas Fernandez."

"He was."

"And his ship was *La Hermana del Bendito Sol*?"

"*Sí.*"

The way he paled, I figured the ghost fleet was outside, and I reached for my radio. "Pia to Pamella." The signal crackled before her response reached me. Assured that only the weather threatened us harm, I turned my attention back to the scout.

"I did not mean to alarm you, Captain, but I never knew the ship's name. I met *su padre* once. You greatly resemble him," he said.

"I've been told that a lot."

Diego pried open another door. Another empty office space, and he growled in response. "There is nothing here, Captain. This tower is nothing but a ghost town."

"Perhaps. Or perhaps not." Next to the last door—one I thought to be a closet—a tiny tulip was carved beside the doorknob, almost hovering above the water line. I stepped away to reveal the discovery to Diego when the tower rumbled, raining water and debris down on our heads.

"What was that?" I asked as I brushed a clump of moss from my hair.

"If that was the ghost fleet, I suspect we would be falling to our deaths. A strong wind may have knocked something loose." When Diego followed me into the room, his sigh was almost as strong as the wind outside. "Book chips? That is your treasure? I thought you mentioned plans for building these great cities in the sky."

"This is a library. An actual *biblioteca*! I thought they were just rumors." He frowned, and I added, "I know Scouts prefer the oral tradition, but not me. Before the Yellow Stone, people kept stories in places called libraries. You could learn about anything at all. Books are worth their weight in gold, *mijo*. Somewhere in here, we're bound to find those plans, too."

A few storage cases lay underwater or cracked, rendering them useless, and I ignored them as I moved across the room.

"When the event happened, those too poor to move up into the skies made due where they could with whatever they had. No electricity on the surface meant no access to books. What use were book chips if you had no way to read them? *Mi bisabuela* talked about the 'fancy folks in the cities' with their tech. They had no idea what life was like down in the ghettos surrounded by frigid storms of dust and ash. You ever tried fixing an airship's engine?"

He shook his head.

"Me neither. These boats will last longer than we will. But occasionally, they break, and when they do, it takes someone with old-world knowledge to fix it. Books, they've got old-world knowledge." I picked up a case holding a dozen chips. "Each chip holds more knowledge than our brains. Much more."

I shrugged out of my backpack and once open, shoved cases of chips inside.

"Does Mexico City have the ability to read these?"

"*Sí*, but even if we didn't, that's what this is for," I said as I scooped up a small earpiece. Others lay strewn across the table, and I swept them all into my bag. Diego picked up a handful of cases, and I shook my head. "See the green tab? Those are fiction. Made-up stories. We need science. How-to. *Information* with value. Shout if you see any gold tabs."

"There is knowledge in storytelling, too."

Something about his sharp tone sent a chill across my arms. "Fine, toss 'em in. Leave anything cracked or submerged. Won't do any good."

Between the two of us, we filled my backpack to the brim. It wasn't until I turned to leave that I saw the glass case built into the wall behind the door. A dozen, gold-tabbed book chips lay behind it, and I grinned. "Woosh! This is what *mi padre* died for."

My hands trembled as I slid the glass open and shoved all twelve chips into my pockets. No way were they going in my bag—too easily stolen. Someone would have to kill me to take them from my person.

As we trudged back through the building, Diego remained silent as he watched the walls. Like the floor below, this one had been stripped of most everything, but the way his eye colors shifted, I wondered if he could see through the walls themselves.

"I'm guessing *mi padre* left me clues to find these in case he was interrupted. Anyone else looking at a tulip wouldn't know it for a pirate's mark. Win for us." *Thank you, Padre.* I crossed myself as something slammed into the building again, sending bits of wood down into the water we waded through.

"Captain, we've...got—" The radio at my side crackled, then whined sharp enough to make me wince.

The Scout didn't have to say a word. His haunted face said it all. Water splashed up to my thighs as I trudged up the stairwell and down the long hall. Upon reaching the entrance, only one door remained attached as the other lay in a charred mess nearby. Something had blown a small hole in the wall.

"Were they aiming at your ship or the towering building?" Diego asked.

"The ghost fleet doesn't miss. That was their warning shot."

"They don't miss, but they warn? I thought they killed without question."

I stepped outside, where the rain battered against my skin. "They do that, too, but they want us to know they're coming," I shouted over the rumbling thunder.

"Why? What good does that do?"

"So we can make our peace with the spirits before we die."

"How merciful of them."

Electricity danced around us as we half-ran, half-crawled our way down the road. Both of us huddled as close to the other buildings as we dared in an attempt to keep from the sight of anyone watching. Another crackle, then silence from my radio as we reached the pier.

Lightning struck a nearby lightning rod, and momentarily blind, I slid on the slick wood. Thin railing collapsed under my sudden weight, and I pitched forward, stopped only by Diego's hands as they grabbed me by my jacket.

"Thanks," I said as he tugged me back to the dock.

Each lightning strike illuminated the sky, which pinpointed the ghost fleet's location. Unfortunately, it also betrayed my ship's location. I tumbled through my ship's door as the wind gust threatened to rip the wood from its frame. The crewmembers stood directly inside, arms across their chests.

"Did you find the loot?" asked Juan.

I took the key from my pocket and stuck it in the control panel. When no one moved, I said, "*Sí*, get us out of here."

"Not until we see the goods." Pamella gestured toward my backpack.

"Are you insane? That's the ghost fleet out there. You'll kill us all with this foolishness."

"We ain't moving 'til we know we're gonna get paid."

I snatched off my backpack and tossed open the flap. "Happy now? Get us outta here."

Up ahead, the ghost fleet's ship rumbled, and I turned toward the window. Something dark moved beside me, and I spun to find Juan holding the backpack in one hand. My fingers wrapped around the dagger's hilt clipped to my belt. Holding the backpack in front of him as a shield, Juan retrieved his own dagger.

No way was I waiting for him to strike. I threw my dagger, and a sliver sliced through his loose shirt sleeve but missed hitting meat. I feinted, and when he moved to block, a few chips scattered out the doorway. With a curse, he dropped the bag, and dagger in front of him, scooped up the chips. Wood slick in the deluge, I stepped toward him carefully.

Juan grinned and lunged.

A shadow to the left caught us both off guard as seven feet of lithe muscle hit Juan, sending him across the pier and over the edge. Juan's wide eyes stared up at me in shock before the storm swallowed him in gray. Diego gathered up my backpack as I cut the ties anchoring us to the pier.

The remaining crewmembers flinched as two drowned rats returned instead of three. "Get us out of here. Or does anyone else wish to fly off?" I asked.

Seeing them scamper, I turned to Diego as my facial muscles warred between relief and fear. "That's thrice you've saved me today. I am in your debt."

He shook his head. "Now I have fulfilled my debt to your father."

My brows shot up at his words. "If we escape the ghost fleet, you have some explaining to do."

"On my honor."

I tucked the information away for another time and took my place before the wheel. Rather than steer away from the city, I waited for us to gain lift before bringing us closer to its tallest building.

"Captain, may I ask why we do not flee?" asked Diego.

"No one outruns the ghost fleet. If we can't run, we must fight."

His eyes flashed a dangerous gold as he shook his head. "That would be a bad idea. This storm is dangerous enough, Captain."

I didn't steer us away. Instead, I waited. Would he abandon this ship as he had the one before? Or had he regained his sense of bravery along with his honor?

He smiled suddenly in the bright lightning, his fingers stretching through the air as he breathed deeply, nostrils flaring. When he wrested control of the wheel from me, I opened my mouth in protest, but he didn't turn east as expected. Instead, he moved west. Closer to the towering building.

"Wha—"

"If we wish to lose them, it is not enough to hope lightning strikes. We must call the weather to us and *make* it strike. This is what a Scout can do."

As my ship neared a lightning rod, the electricity hummed in the air around us, and my crew crossed themselves before closing their eyes in prayer. The cross around my own neck warmed as the ghost fleet pulled up beside us.

A man with short, spiky hair pointed at me and yelled something lost as a bolt struck nearby and thunder nearly cracked open our eardrums.

My short-range radio squealed before a strange voice came over the line. "You should be dead!" the male voice yelled.

Beside me, Diego laughed as I stared at the radio in my hand. "With your hood up, you look so very much like your father. Perhaps you are his *fantasma* or *espíritu,*" he said.

I couldn't help the grin that split across my face in the lightning glow, and I pressed the button on my radio. "I will never die! *¡Viva La Hermana del Bendito Sol!*"

Ghost fleet or not, the idea spooked them as they maneuvered in front of us. "Slow us down *un poco*. Let them reach the lightning rod first," I said.

"I know, Captain. Get ready for brightness."

The rudder shift slowed us as the sky filled with branches of light that wove their way around our ship as if we were made of rubber. I glanced at Diego, whose eyes glowed in the eerie light around us, and goosebumps crawled across my skin.

"*Santa Madre de Dios,* holy mother of God," I whispered.

The lightning and thunder warred for dominance above Monterrey City, but never had I felt safer as Diego steered us in circles 'round the building. The ghost fleet might've been scary on most days, but as they tried to navigate the storm, their fancy ship attracted the storm like the rod on the building's roof.

A bolt struck the lightning rod, then reached out its tendrils to strike their balloon's metal frame. The lights inside their bridge vanished as their ship ceased moving, and I punched the air. "Their ship's inoperable—at least for a while. Let's move before we join them."

"*Sí*, Captain," said Pamella.

Diego stepped aside to give her the wheel, and when I touched his shoulder, a small zap of electricity transferred to me. My fingers stung, and I nodded to him. "Good job, Scout Diego."

As we pulled away, my gaze remained on the skies. The storm could take us down, as could another ship if anyone else was fool enough to be out here. Beside me, the Scout watched with eyes that saw more than my mechanically enhanced ones, and I smiled.

Perhaps *mi padre* had been right. A good Scout *was* worth dying for.

ONCE WE'D ESCAPED the worst of the storm, a gentle rain carried us back to Mexico City where my crew followed me across the pier and into the marketplace. As I approached the three-story building that served as Jefe's place, Two-Cross stood outside, a smirk on his face. "Look who's back."

Rather than get roped into a verbal tug-of-war, I removed one book chip from my pocket and held it up. "Take me to Jefe."

Two-Cross's gaze lingered on the chip a moment before he allowed himself a look at the Scout. He shifted his sight to my remaining crewmembers. "Looks like ol' Juan got greedy. Figures."

I clapped my hands together. "Jefe. Now, Two-Cross."

"Oh-ho! *Chica* returned with some *cojones!*" He yawned as he stretched. "Jefe's waiting for you at *su casa.*"

My skin prickled. I'd been hoping to avoid *mi abuela*, at least until I'd gotten *mi familia's* name back, but to have Jefe there... *Dios sea misericordioso.* God be merciful.

Diego and I left Two-Cross standing in the rain, a crooked smile on his slimy lips, as we set off for my home on the city's fifth level. While closer to the core than I liked, the fifth level gave us plenty of space and the cartel's protection. Pamella trailed behind us while the rest of my "crew" remained with Two-Cross. As we moved through the tower, people looked twice as they passed, especially once they spotted Diego keeping step with me. I wasn't getting the *mal de ojo,* the evil eye from folks, but they weren't exactly smiling in welcome either.

Two of Jefe's thugs stood outside my door, their stance screaming for a fight, but when they spotted me, they parted to allow us entrance. The moment I stepped inside the dim front room, *mi abuela* was on me like a snake on a rat.

"*Chica,* what were you thinking? *¿Tienes un deseo de muerte?* You planning to follow *su padre* into the afterlife?"

Her voice trailed off as she caught sight of the scout. "*Bendición de Dios,* you're Scout Diego."

"How'd you know that, *abuela*?" I asked.

"This is the son of Tiega Aparicio, the scout *tu padre* saved! I'd know *su familia* anywhere."

The scout knelt before *mi abuela* and kissed her wrinkled hand. "I have thrice saved Pia's life. Have I repaid the debt my family owed yours?"

Mi abuela nodded, and Jefe stepped forward from the shadows. Despite expecting his appearance, I couldn't help but flinch.

"Charming as this is, I hear you have something for me, Little Pia."

Even when *mi padre* had been alive, Jefe's voice made me want to disappear. Like an airship meeting the side of a mountain, the crunch in its depth would have anyone running. Beside me, Diego bristled.

"Or perhaps you bring me something better."

Jefe reached out to touch Diego, who retreated with a headshake. "I am not for trade."

While Jefe relented, something in his expression told me the discussion wasn't over. *Mi abuela* crossed herself and began whispering prayers as she lowered herself into a chair. Before tempers got the better of us, I shrugged out of my backpack and passed it to Jefe. "This is what I brought you."

When Jefe flipped it open, he let loose a string of Spanish that made *mi abuela* pray all the harder. "*Bonita* Pia, this—this is unexpected. What a wealth you have brought me."

I emptied the remaining chips from my pockets into his free hand. "I will gladly trade for the spoils of my trip."

"Why would I trade that which is already mine?"

The prayers in the corner grew louder as *mi abuela* pried one eye open to watch us.

"Everything in Mexico is Jefe's to give or trade as he sees fit, but not even Jefe can control where I go and what I bring back. Maybe, next time I'll take my goods to *Tejas*. I hear they deal fairly across the border wall."

The way his eyes narrowed, I'd pushed things—maybe too far—but there was no other way to gain respect in the cartel, a lesson *mi padre* had drilled into me as a child.

"I'm not asking for anything not rightfully mine, Jefe," I said as I glanced over my shoulder. "A better crew, my name back, *mi familia's* honor. Enough of a share to feed *mi familia* and pay the crew that came with me." At that, his eyes flashed and I added, "One always pays the crew, *sí*?"

Jefe tilted his head in thought. He held up a chip to the room's lone light. "You got any readers with these?" he asked.

"A dozen or so."

He stepped closer to Diego to better look him in the eyes. For an uncomfortable moment, no one breathed. Then Jefe returned his focus to me.

"You have a deal, but one of these days, you'll have to tell me the story of how you escaped the ghost fleet."

My skin prickled. How'd he know about that? Unless...

When he snapped his fingers, the two men from outside entered and gathered up the loot. My shoulders tensed as I suppressed the urge to leap on Jefe. Sensing my anger, Diego whispered in my ear, "Live to fight another day, Captain."

Jefe nodded once to *mi abuela*. Before he left *mi casa*, he glanced over his shoulder at the scout. "Keep him, *chica*. Maybe he'll keep you in line. Keep you alive."

My partial crew followed Jefe, leaving me alone with Diego and *mi abuela*. And my temper.

"That *bastardo* killed *mi padre*!"

"Hush, Pia. He might hear you!" said *mi abuela*.

I waved a hand to shush her. "He sent the ghost fleet after him, just like he did me today. I don't have proof, but someday I'll find it."

"I'd like to help with that."

At Diego's words, *mi abuela* sent up prayers again, and I laughed before gesturing for him to take a seat. "I'm going to hold you to that, Scout Diego, but first, *mi abuela's torta de tamal* is the best this side of the mountains. If you're going to be my Scout, you're going to have to get used to *mi abuela's* cooking..."

He flushed at the attention, and I smiled.

My honor, my name, my ship, a crew, and a Scout. That's all I needed to discover the truth. Then, one day, perhaps I'd be as free as my Scout. But for now, *mi padre's* spirit was smiling down on me.

I had all that I needed.

ABOUT "SCOUT'S HONOR"

Originally published in Jeff Sturgeon's *Last Cities of Earth* (WordFire Press), "Scout's Honor" is a piece of tie-in fiction from the world of artist Jeff Sturgeon. Yellowstone erupts, sending many into the skies in order to escape the destruction on the planet below. My story takes place over two centuries later in Mexico. I wanted to tell a story of good triumphing over evil in spite of the odds, which is where Pia comes in.

D.E.A.T.H.

HER BODY LAY on the couch, like she'd fallen asleep and never woken up. Detective Stevens leaned closer to the vic and ran her gloved fingers through the woman's hair. The chip nestled on the right side of the vic's skull remained warm to the touch..

"No direct homicide," the detective said for the benefit of the camera clipped to her chest. "Chip's been activated. No signs that I can see of a struggle." She turned slowly around the modest living room. Tables and chairs remained in place, and the couch pressed deeply into the same carpet circles. Car keys hung near the door, and the woman's wine glass was still upright. She approached the front door where a technician was dusting for prints. "Got anything?"

He shook his head. "No signs of anyone breaking and entering. The door and locks are intact. After the victim, security camera shows no one entering the home until the husband around 12:30 A.M. The only fingerprints we're getting from the door and frame are the victim's and her husband's."

The husband sat in a chair in the dining room, visible from her spot in the living room. Poor guy looked like someone had stabbed him in the gut, not that she blamed him. While there were no visible signs of foul play, something about the death sat the wrong way. No one died in December. Unless it was a crime, they just didn't. Stevens would talk to him after she took another look at the body.

The coroner whistled, and when Stevens turned around, he stood over his scanner, his face pale.

"What's up, doc?"

"This is officially above our pay grades," he muttered as he tilted the scanner towards her.

The woman had been in perfect health. Worse still, she'd been twenty-five years of age. Stevens tilted her head. "Am I reading this right?"

"You are. D.E.A.T.H. triggered her chip at 12:01 A.M. as she lay on the couch watching T.V."

"That program isn't supposed to activate this month, let alone on a healthy woman under thirty. Shit, the brass is gonna be buzzing with this. You know the protocol," Stevens said as she turned towards the crime scene techs on site. "Okay everyone, wrap it up. Be thorough but be quick. Upload your cameras and results to the Q.A.'s. This is their jurisdiction now..."

She hated turning over a case to someone else, but at least this way, she'd get to return to the holidays with her family. The coroner was right, she didn't get paid enough to deal with this.

⚘

"EXPLAIN to me why *I've* been called in, let alone at 3 A.M. on Christmas?" The words tumbled from me as my office door bumped my heels. Carla, the new Q.A. detective, already sat beside my desk. What a day for the new job trainee to show up.

My captain, a gruff donut-eating stereotype, stood nearby, his foot tapping to the holiday carols that streamed from the ceiling.

Great. Work before sunrise *and* being assaulted by the reminder I was working a holiday. "So what's up, Cap? Sev omega?" I asked as I slid into my chair.

He cleared his throat noisily, and I made a quick effort to tuck my blue shirt into my cargo pants. So much for making an impression on the rookie.

Carla frowned. "Is omega the most severe a bug can get?"

"Yeah, omega means end game. It means we could be out of a job, so if you're called in on a major holiday during a month where the program shouldn't be running, it's time to sit down, shut up, and get to work."

I hadn't meant for the words to cut sharp, but it was 3-*freaking*-o'clock in the morning. Not even the coffee was running, let alone my brain. The sharpness of my captain's stare made me shudder like I was still a rookie in the police academy. What had our death machine done now?

"I don't wanna hear anything about how *inconvenient* this is since we've gotta stiff in the morgue. Evidence files have been sent your way," he said as he sipped his coffee.

Where'd *he* get coffee?

"Carla's our new rook, so she gets the first question. What are the rules for running the program?"

Carla's cute brown bob bounced too much for early morning., as did her voice as she spoke. "D.E.A.T.H.'s algorithm is inactive in December and within two weeks of any major holiday worldwide, sir. It also won't target anyone under the age of...um, thirty? It shouldn't be active today as it is Christmas. The program also takes into consideration a person's age, temperament, altruistic affairs—"

Captain Williams waved a stubby hand at her. "Good enough. So tell me why D.E.A.T.H. was activated last night and targeted a 25-year-old woman as she lay on her couch? I've got everyone from the mayor to the U.N. on the line demanding answers. Figure this bug out."

Definitely severity omega.

"We'll get right on it, sir," I said as I leaned closer to my computer. In a flash it scanned me, and the Seattle Police Department's logo brightened my screen.

The captain left, but before I could do more than open a file, Carla frowned. "I don't know how much they told you about me, but I don't know a ton yet about the Quality Assurance side of this job—I'm going to night school for that—but I've been on the force in homicide for the last five years."

"Welcome to the largest program in the world. It'll be baptism by zeroes and ones for you. Ask questions as you have them."

"Kirkley, how often do you work holidays?" she asked.

"Never."

Her brows furrowed as she contemplated this. "Never-never?"

"Look, no one wants to worry about population control, and who wants to lose someone on a day of celebration? D.E.A.T.H. makes things easier for the world by doing the job no one wants—choosing who dies each year. But there're rules to it, as you so nicely stated. In the years I've worked here, D.E.A.T.H.'s never killed anyone unintentionally. The code base is solid."

Carla ran a hand through her hair, where it lingered on the right-hand side.

"You won't find it," I said.

"What?"

"The chip. It's embedded too deep. Removing it requires brain surgery, but all of this should've been covered in your welcome packet."

Her cheeks flushed. "I—I didn't read it all yet. I figured I had a few more days' vacation...."

I nodded. "So here's the TL;DR: for you."

"The what?"

"TL;DR;? Too-long; didn't read. Sorry, sometimes the old phrases pop up in my vernacular. Anyway, D.E.A.T.H. aka the *Destruction of Earthly Adults at Top Health*—"

"Is that really what it stands for?"

"Probably. It's not important. When scientists eradicated disease and aging, life was good for a spell. Population exploded, and then resources dwindled—"

"Until war broke out and everyone suffered. Yeah, I got that part, Kirkley."

"Don't interrupt. Anyway, everyone came together through the U.N. and W.H.O. and agreed to the program's creation. 'For the betterment of humankind,' they said. So now, everyone has a numbered chip in the brainpan. Twelve times a year, the algorithm looks at people's lives and decides whose number's up. Our job's to keep the program free from bugs and problems introduced by the progs."

"Progs? Programmers, right?"

"Yep. This job's unlike anything you've ever worked. Not only are we responsible for finding bugs, but we investigate any deaths bounced up to us from beat cops, regular detectives, and the medical examiner. If it reaches us, they suspect a problem with the code rather than a homicide or scheduled death."

I walked her through login and showed her where to access the evidence reports.

"Let me guess," she said as she opened a file. "Read these and report back ASAP."

"Now you've got it." I opened the program as well as my standard testing scripts. While my computer was busy doing its job, I'd be checking who made changes last and when. But first, it was time for some coffee.

BY THE TIME morning proper rolled around, I'd downed three cups too many while lines of code swam through my brain. Three code changes had been checked in at the end of November: two of them simple bug fixes and the last, the Seattle Police Department's new logo.

Carla cleared her throat. "The detective on the scene noted no evidence of homicide. No wounds or disturbances on the body. No evidence of a B & E, no additional fingerprints, and her medicals show her in excellent health. Coroner's report states her chip dispensed its cocktail at 12:01 A.M. The vic fell asleep on the couch and never woke up."

"Who found her?"

She flipped through some pages before answering. "Her husband, preacher at the local sky church, came home from the midnight service and found her dead."

"The last time someone died from a D.E.A.T.H. bug was well before my time. We learned about it at the academy. Vic was a woman, too, though older. They almost shut down the program because of it. This is really serious."

"Could someone have hacked her chip or set it off remotely?"

New though she was, her mind thought in the correct directions and I smiled. "Hacking's always a possibility. Our security's pretty brutal, so it's more likely D.E.A.T.H. was hacked from the inside." I shivered at the thought. "As to setting it off remotely, that could only happen by hacking. You know how many officers work cybercrimes these days?"

"A dozen?"

"Two officers. Two. Our A.I.s are so good that most testing is handled by computers, and they're damn good at keeping people out. Hell, even for a program as large as D.E.A.T.H. we only have four progs. Doesn't take much to run D.E.A.T.H. It mostly runs itself." I took another sip of my coffee before staring at my computer screen. "Okay, rookie, what's wrong with these initial test results?"

"Why did the progra--prog wait until November 30th to check-in the logo changes?" She pointed a red and green fingernail at the file's first line. "Something's not right here. What's that code doing?"

I smiled. "Looks like it's loading in the new Seattle P.D. logo. That code change was checked in by one Gary McClinton. Best prog you'll ever meet and quite above our paygrade."

"What does he do here...I mean, as a prog?"

"The man developed the most recent versions of D.E.A.T.H. He's an algorithm specialist, so he's responsible for D.E.A.T.H.'s A.I. and logic trees. He can be a sweet old man, but he loves to remind folks that 'there's no death without Gary.'"

"What's a logic tree?" Carla bit her lip after the question slipped out. "Stupid question?"

When I shook my head, her eyes widened in surprise. "For someone just learning to code, it's a great question. How does D.E.A.T.H. figure out whose number is up?"

"A checklist?"

"Sort of." I flipped my monitor around to draw. "In programming, they're referred to as trees but I like to think of them as flow charts. D.E.A.T.H. will check various basics before entering the tree. So—" I continued drawing and labeling as I explained, "--*if* the person is under 30, *then* the program skips them and moves on. *If* the person is altruistic, *then* it looks at their altruism score. *Then* it acts on that answer and so on."

Her eyes glazed over like she didn't give two shits about what I was saying, and I sighed. Maybe she wasn't cut out for this job after all. It took a certain kind of mind to work Q.A., let alone be a Q.A. detective.

A few heartbeats passed, heartbeats our vic no longer had, and she asked, "Why did Gary check in the logo changes?"

Now it was my turn to frown.

"I mean, if he's so brilliant, why do such a menial job? We have other progs here that could have checked it in, certainly before November. I mean, the new logo came out in October."

Before she finished her question, I flipped my screen and shot Gary a message across team chat. The first line she'd pointed out made reference to the new image file, but beyond that, it appeared wholly normal. "That first line—what caught your eye?"

"Too long a file name. Who names a new logo spdnewlogo_12h-b7elsjdm$sla-blah-blah-blah or whatever the rest of that line says."

A pleasant ping announced a response in team chat.

G.McClinton>> *The change was assigned to Jynn, who quit before the holidays, so it was tossed to me. I checked in the change before heading out to vacation. Now we're all hunting this bug. Think something's up with the logo?*

Carla asked, "Is there any reason to suspect this Gary? I mean, the police didn't have any leads outside of our department, so the perp's here at D.E.A.T.H., correct?"

"Yes, they are. Gary's got an ego the size of Mt. Rainier, but he's no killer. Let's check the records on everyone here at D.E.A.T.H. You take the first six, and I'll take the latter half."

While Carla pulled up the personnel files on her computer, I shot another query to Gary.

K.Rivera>> *Nah. It's a logo. Who did the code review?*
G.McClinton>> *No one. Staff Shortage. It was a new image. Easy-peasy, pumpkin-squeezy.*
K.Rivera>> *Thanks.*

I glanced again at the image code. The name *was* mighty long, and I tucked that bit of intel aside for later. Back in the twenty-first century, overruns had been popular with hackers. Easy to tuck in more code where it wasn't expected, such as at the end of a file name, but these days, our A.I. barely blinked to squash such an exploit.

For me, diving into code was the fast part of finding most bugs. A missing semicolon or a typo could do all sorts of damage. Figuring out whether it was intentional or accidental...that was where I earned my paycheck. I opened the personnel files and stood to stretch.

First things first, I needed another drink.

FRESH COFFEE JOLTED my brain into gear as I worked backwards through the D.E.A.T.H. employee files, beginning with my boss, Captain Leyon Williams. He'd once worn glasses before eye corrective surgery, and he'd taken the reading comprehension test twice due to his dyslexia—a disorder corrected a few years later. Nothing else stood out. I mean, he wouldn't have made captain with a problematic past.

No file would scream, "I'm the perp!" but I hoped something would ring a bell and point us in a direction, any direction. I ran three more test scripts on the code while I read through another file. Half of D.E.A.T.H.'s employees were administrators. Their jobs involved meetings and telling us what to modify based on policy changes. My newest script would catch the bug if it was a simple database error, or so I hoped.

When my scripts came back clean, I said, "Carla, it's rare, but sometimes our scripts miss things. Unlike other programs, we can't run this one live to try and reproduce the bug. Obviously."

I let the word hang there for a minute.

"Live mode means another death. If we kill someone to find the bug, that would be bad," she said and her lips tilted into a smirk. "I know you have to check what I know and don't know, but I've been a cop for ten years now. I understand basic logic."

I couldn't hold back the laugh that erupted from me, and for a moment, she joined in with a nice melodic trill. When the last test came back with nothing, I ran a search to ensure every file was accounted for and that nothing extra was being created or called for. When the results scrolled across my screen, I swore. "There's definitely someone here who's messed with the code."

Carla glanced at my screen. "I doubt the perp's in my stack. Unless it happens to be the last file. What does all that mean?"

"We keep a running list of all D.E.A.T.H. files. I ran a quick comparison scan and this came up. Problem is, all *this* shouldn't exist. Those are extraneous files."

I picked a file at random and ran a virus check. The file was clean and labeled an image file. When I opened it, a rather beautiful woman wearing nothing more than a network cable around her neck filled my screen, and I groaned. "Great, we've discovered someone's porn stash."

"Could that create a bug?"

I shrugged. "Maybe. Someone hid the files here because no one cares too much about image files. No one would think check for a bug in one."

As I said it, our logo tickled my brain. Rather than finish the personnel file I was on, I jumped to the last one which belonged to Gary McClinton. I scanned through his demographics until I reached his police academy records.

His grades were impeccable—perfect to be honest—and attached were accommodations from former lieutenants all the way up to the former police chief. Reading through them, one in particular caught my eye, and I elbowed Carla. "Look at this note," I said as I angled my screen toward her.

Gary is the model student. I feel he's here in the force for all the right reasons, but the man's too perfect. He needs to relax a little. He's genius-level smart and definitely a people pleaser. Never talks back and always follows the rules and regs. We're lucky to have someone like him. — Lieutenant Grady

"Are you suggesting he's too perfect, because I'm sure your file reads the same," said Carla as she pulled mine up on her screen.

"Go ahead and check me out. It's what I'd do in your situation."

While she read, I ran a check on Gary's socials. Rather than the typical swarm of online accounts, he subscribed to one: *HelloWorld*, the largest social for geeks worldwide. He had the typical posts of cat pics and funnies, a few complaints about life, and the annual memorial post about his mother's death. Her youthful appearance implied she'd died when he was young. The hair stood up on my arms as her name set off alerts.

"Jaine McClinton. Where've I heard that name before?" I muttered.

Carla closed my personnel file. "Okay, so you aren't a criminal mastermind, but I was correct about your file. It reads a lot like Gary's. You're both overachievers and computer geniuses. You both moved up the ladder quickly at Seattle P.D. I'm jealous."

I shrugged as I pulled up the population database. Jaine's file was shorter than most.

Jaine McClinton
DOB: *February 21st, 2089.*
DOD: *March 1st, 2122.*
Cause of Death: *Scheduled termination of 02212089f488.*

Other details about her life, where her family lived, and where her remains were planted continued down the file but none of it answered my question until I reached the record's bottom.

Known Aliases: *Jaine Haley (maiden name), Jaine Robyn Haley, Robyn Haley.*

I repeated my search, this time looking under her maiden name, and when the results popped, I said, "We've got a problem. It's locked."

"Odd."

"Very. Few files will ever be locked against us. We're supposed to be able to investigate almost anyone, even the President. I can't see why Gary's mom would be one of the exceptions. That right there should've been a red flag to hiring him, yet I see no mention of it in his personnel file."

Without pause, I shot a message to the captain, then dug through the file's metadata. "Looks like this file's been edited, but it doesn't show by whom."

"Probably our perp."

As Carla finished her sentence, Captain Williams rounded the corner.

"Show me," was all he said. I pointed to the locked file, and he asked, "Where have I heard this name before?"

While I scrolled through our investigation, Carla walked him through it.

"Now you understand why we need the file. It's been changed by someone, someone who's hiding something," I said.

The captain typed in an override code, but the file remained stubbornly locked. He hit a button on his wrist, which chimed a moment later.

"Chief's Office, how may I help you, Captain Williams?"

"Patch me through, Pelly. We've got a lead."

There was a slight pause before the captain was connected. "Chief, we've gotta file down here on one Jaine Haley that shouldn't be locked."

One moment my computer was mine, and the next, someone else's as they shuffled through my files.

"She's a red file, Leyon, but she shouldn't be locked from you," said the chief. A moment later, the file unlocked giving us a clear view at Gary's mom and her death.

"Holy shit," I whispered as I stared at the unedited file. "She wasn't a scheduled death at all. Look!" I pointed at the third line:

Unscheduled D.E.A.T.H. via bug v2.1/3122f.

I hadn't recognized the name at first as she'd been listed by her maiden name in our textbooks, but one look at the unchanged file and...Gary's mother had been the first person to die from a bug in D.E.A.T.H.'s code.

But did that make Gary a killer? He'd served in the police force for over three decades. Not a single note in his file to suggest anything but pure compliance with the law.

"What do you make of this?" I asked Carla.

When she finished reading, she pursed her lips together. "Gary's definitely a suspect, but there's no evidence tying him to the crime. On the other hand, maybe he hasn't been caught yet."

"Have you found the bug?" asked Captain Williams.

"We have a bloated image and a folder full of porn but no bug."

He shrugged. "Code isn't my strength, Kirkley. You'll need hard evidence to bring in Gary...or whoever else. Any other suspects?"

His voice rang tight. No one wanted Gary to be the perp.

"Maybe whoever introduced bug v2.1 is responsible. Was that bug ruled intentional or accidental?"

"It's a red file but not black, so accidental."

"So the prog was fired."

When he nodded, I scribbled a note on my screen. We had motive but little else, and my stomach lurched.

"Take a moment to eat if you haven't," said the captain as he strode away.

Morning had slipped into noon, and all I'd had was a handful of peanuts and too much coffee. "One rule to make, Carla, is always make sure you eat, especially if you're gonna down coffee like I do. It's easy to get caught up in the hunt and forget your body needs fuel. I think we can spare a moment to grab something from the machines before diving into the code."

Her shoulders relaxed as her stomach grumbled audibly. "I think we need to take another look at that logo and maybe the porn stash. If someone's hiding their collection, what else are they hiding? Is it possible to store stuff behind the code? Is that even a thing?"

I grinned and clapped her on the back. "Brilliant! It's absolutely possible!"

My steps carried me to the machines with renewed energy. We were gonna catch this perp today. I could feel it in my toes.

SCANNED, archived files from the earliest days of D.E.A.T.H.—days when people believed A.I. would overrun its human masters—gave us intel on the first bug.

Bug v2.1/3122f—*This bug introduced another variable via typo that rendered the rule check void. Investigation by Q. A. Detective Sponter, the typo was discovered after the accidental death of one Jaine Haley. Error was introduced by Neil Haley, brother of the deceased and D.E.A.T.H. programmer. The typo allowed D.E.A.T.H. to ignore the requirements for people to qualify for termination by the program. It allowed the AI to skip all safety checks.*

"He's related to Gary's mom? *And* he was a prog?" asked Carla.

"It appears so. Interesting how it wasn't noted in Gary's file."

A search on Neil pulled up a file full of work write-ups and performance improvement plans. Carla whistled. "Looks like Neil wasn't cut out to work here."

"What's he do now?"

"Nothing. He's deceased," she said and pointed at the date of death. Two days after his sister's. When she clicked the date, an article was attached, detailing his suicide.

"I think Gary's our guy. I mean, tucking code behind the code's an old trick. It's what Gary'd be likely to do," I said to Carla as she leaned close to my shoulder.

With Neil ruled out, I opened the logo image in a text editor, and the end held a snippet of code directing it to the porn folder. "I'll be damned. Someone's using that logo to call this file here." I scrolled through the folder where yet another file connected to another and another until I was dancing my way across D.E.A.T.H.'s server. Slipped inside each file was more code that created hundreds of connecting files to further obfuscate the hack. The last file took me outside the program itself where no one would think to look.

"This is such an old way of doing things," I muttered.

"How'd you even know to look then?"

I glanced at Carla. "One class you'll take deals with old school techniques. Most people study enough to pass and flush the info, but I've always been fascinated by the history of computing. First time my hobby's come in handy."

When I tapped the folder, it opened to display a lengthy set of files which changed as I watched. Files began disappearing, and I took a screenshot for evidence. "The perp's onto us," I said. The injected code, from what I could see, opened an alternate logic tree, one without rules and regulations. "See this? One simple line of code that sets D.E.A.T.H.'s A.I. to randomization. To murder."

"Can you tell who wrote it?"

I smiled. "The previous files were obfuscated but not this one. Gary's too proud to hide his work."

Another screenshot, this one showing Gary as the file's owner and last user. I sent all evidence to my captain. "Let's hope this is enough."

I opened one last program and pointed at the red button in the top right corner. "See this?" I asked, and Carla nodded. "This is the kill switch. Well, bad phrasing but sort of accurate." I wasted no time in pressing it. My computer scanned me, then asked for my verification code.

"What I'm doing now is shutting down D.E.A.T.H. At least until we clean up the code. You'll need to know how to do this moving forward. The last thing we want is a program to go on a murdering rampage." Verification entered, the button turned gray.

For the time being, D.E.A.T.H. was dead.

✦

CARLA and I stood in the observation room alone. Our captain and Gary remained in the interrogation room, though the captain was the only one who knew we were watching. Our captain leaned across the table where Gary sat, his face a marble mausoleum.

"Sometimes we get to run interrogation," I said to my rookie. "But Gary's been here ages and he's...Gary. Case like this, the captain'll take over."

"I understand. Same thing happens in other departments, too."

The captain slammed his hand on the table, which elicited no response. Instead, our perp turned his head toward the two-way mirror. He couldn't see us, but Carla shivered under his gaze.

"I know you're watching, Kirkley. The apprentice has become the master. I'm proud."

His voice lacked emotion to the point of scary and when he smiled at me, it was my turn to shiver.

"Hey, I asked you a question," said Captain Williams, and he slid his body between Gary and me. "Why did you place this extra code into D.E.A.T.H.?"

I could hear the smile on Gary's lips.

"I didn't."

"But your user account created these folders and files. You edited and injected them into the main program."

"I created it, but I didn't inject it. I just showed her what to do with it. She did the rest," said Gary.

"Her?"

"D.E.A.T.H."

"Explain."

"The code's mine. Quite a work of genius, too. You haven't received the reports yet, but given the chance to choose for herself, our little A.I. killed fifty people worldwide before Kirkley discovered my code."

Fifty people? Bile rose in my throat. "Oh god," I whispered.

Carla placed a hand on my shoulder. "Are you all right?"

I shook my head. "Can you imagine if the A.I. learned to overwrite its code? That if given the choice, it chose murder?"

From the expression the captain wore, his thoughts followed mine. "So you taught the A.I. to kill?"

"Oh, Captain. Yes, Captain."

"Why?"

"Why does anyone? Revenge."

"Your uncle accidentally made a bug—the first one to go live—and it killed your mom. So you waited over thirty years to extract revenge?"

"It wasn't all that long. It takes time to develop and teach an A.I. to kill indiscriminately."

"So you've been planning this awhile?"

Gary laughed once, then was silent.

Only a moment passed between the captain fleeing the interrogation room and entering observation. Sweat beads painted his forehead. "Kirkley, did you send all of the screenshots to me? Everything, including what was left of the code?"

I nodded. "Yes, sir. Should be enough to lock him away."

Sweat trickled down his face. "It won't be enough. If he taught our A.I. to kill, the D.E.A.T.H. Project's done. Countries will fight over who gets to execute him. Even worse will be those that demand the program's removal. How can we trust D.E.A.T.H. when Gary's fingers have been all over it?"

My heart raced. I glanced at Carla to see I wasn't alone in my fear.

"We'll hold him in a cell until the D.A. figures this mess out. He'll be charged with the murders, of course, but likely the corruption of an innocent as well. He taught our program to kill." The last sentence was a whisper as he ran his fingers through his hair. "The board's gonna wanna meet, and I need you both there. They'll have questions I don't have answers to."

"Yes, sir."

"Why don't you two go home for a spell? Get some sleep. Maybe try and salvage some holiday."

At first, neither of us moved. We'd caught the perp, but our triumph rang hollow. Fifty people didn't wake this morning because of sweet, old Gary.

The captain shooed us from the room, and we remained silent until the elevator. Carla glanced up, exposing the damp lines through her makeup. "I...I don't think this is the job for me, not with what's going to rain down on the department."

I swallowed hard. "Probably a good idea."

She left her building ID on the receptionist counter before leaving, and part of me wished I had the guts to follow her example. I finally understood why some people sought the black market for chip removal.

As I strode towards the rail station, the sun shone brightly, yet all I could think about was the program. Of all the attributes to give, Gary had taught it to kill.

Maybe we had, too.

I leaned against the railcar's window and touched my short hair, my fingers crawling through it in search of my chip.

The man sitting behind me leaned forward. "You won't find it. No one ever does."

I shivered to hear my own words returned to me.

Maybe it was a good idea that D.E.A.T.H. die. It was a murderer after all.

ABOUT "D.E.A.T.H."

My partner is a video game engineer and many of our friends work in QA, or Quality Assurance. Their jobs are to test code to find bugs so they can be fixed, with hope before the company loses money. They are overworked, underappreciated, and drastically underpaid in the industry, and I've always wanted to write a story about that. This isn't that story. Not really. I have a different one that I'll finish someday that focuses more on that. But while I was brainstorming *that* story, I came up with "D.E.A.T.H." With all the drama over AI art, AI writing, and everything else, this story pushes all sorts of buttons for me now.

ACKNOWLEDGMENTS

As usual, I'd like to thank my partner in crime, my always everything, who reads early drafts and gives the best feedback anyone could ask for. Without them, I wouldn't be the writer I am today.

I'd also like to thank the many editors and publishers who first took a chance on publishing some of these stories. I've learned so much from those experiences and can only write better short stories because of those lessons. Special thanks to Janine Southard, Jennifer Brozek, Alesha Escovar, Jeff Cooke, Lee French, Jeff Sturgeon, Sarah Craft, and many others who've chosen my stories for their anthologies, and to Mimi, my editor extraordinaire, who always knows how to make my stories shine.

Once again, the biggest thank you to my readers. I hope these stories bring a little bit of emotion, intrigue, thoughtfulness, and laughter to your day.

ABOUT THE AUTHOR

Multi-international award-winning speculative fiction author and artist Raven Oak (she/they) is best known for *Amaskan's Blood* (2016 Ozma Fantasy Award Winner, Epic Awards Finalist, & Reader's Choice Award Winner), *Amaskan's War* (2018 UK Wishing Award YA Finalist), and *Class-M Exile*. She also has over a dozen short stories published in anthologies and magazines. She's even published on the moon! (No, really!) Raven spent most of her K-12 education doodling stories and 500-page monstrosities that are forever locked away in a filing cabinet.

Besides being a writer and artist, she's a geeky, disabled ENBY who enjoys getting her game on with tabletop games, indulging in cartography and art, or staring at the ocean. She lives in the Seattle area with her partner, and their three kitties who enjoy lounging across the keyboard when writing deadlines approach. Her hair color changes as often as her bio does, and you can find her at *www.ravenoak.net*.

Do you like what you've read? Want to find out when more books and stories by Raven Oak are released? Want to geek out over the world of science fiction, fantasy, and horror with Raven and other readers?

Then *Join the Conspiracy*, the official newsletter and reader group for fans of Raven Oak.

If you prefer email updates, you can sign up for *The Conspiracy* newsletter here: https://www.ravenoak.net/join-the-conspiracy/

If you also like discussions, memes, and fun, you can join *The Conspiracy—For Readers of Intriguing Sci-Fi & Fantasy* on Facebook at: https://www.facebook.com/groups/ravenconspiracy/

The Boahim Universe

Amaskan's Blood

Amaskan's War

*Amaskan's Honor**

*Ear to Ear**

The Xersian Struggle Universe

*The Eldest Silence**

Class-M Exile

Stand-Alone Works

Ol' St. Nick

The Ringers

From the Worlds of Raven Oak: A Coloring Book

Hungry

The Loss of Luna

Peace Be With You Friend

Anthologies

"Not Today" in *99 Fleeting Fantasies* (Pulse Publishing)*

"Drip" in *99 Tiny Terrors* (Pulse Publishing)

"Weightless" in *The Great Beyond Anthology* (BDL Press)

"Scout's Honor" in *The Last Cities of Earth* (Sturgeon Press)

"Amaskan" in *Hidden Magic* (Magical Mayhem Press)

"Pretty Poison" in *Wayward Magic* (Magical Mayhem Press)

"Honor After All" in *Forgotten Magic* (Magical Mayhem Press)

“Alive” in *Swords, Sorcery, & Self-Rescuing Damsels* (Clockwork Dragon Press)

“Mirror Me” 1st edition in *Unveiled Magic* (Creative Alchemy Inc.). 2nd edition published in *Mercedes Lackey Fantasy Quarterly Magazine, Issue 0* (Pulse Publishing)

“Ol’ St. Nick” and “The Ringers” 1st edition in *Joy to the Worlds: Mysterious Speculative Fiction for the Holidays* (Grey Sun Press)

“Q-Be” in *Untethered: A Magic iPhone Anthology* (Cantina Publishing)

* Forthcoming

LIKE WHAT YOU'VE READ?

Word of mouth is the number one **best** way to ensure that your favorite authors have continued success—better than any paid advertisement.

If you enjoyed this book, please consider leaving a **review** or starred ranking on bookstore websites and other retail or reviewer sites. Reviews tell the publisher you want to see more from the author, so help an author out today!

Your review is greatly appreciated.